WILD PRIDE

THE HONEYWELLS OF KENTUCKY, BOOK 3

VANESSA GRAY BARTAL

DRY CREEK PRESS

CHAPTER 1

*D*arcy Honeywell was a ladies' man, at least as much as any Honeywell was. He cycled through women at an almost alarming rate. Contrary to popular belief, he really did want to settle down. The problem was that he was looking for perfection, and he couldn't find it.

His standards were exacting, but forever was a long time. Darcy wanted to make sure he was with the right person. To him, the right person was tall. At 6'10", he was the second-tallest brother. Maybe his siblings were content to be with pint-sized women, but he wasn't. Though he would never say as much to Corliss and Brent, when they stood next to their mates, they looked like giants. For his part, Darcy wasn't willing to accept anyone under 5'10". That still left a gap of a foot, but after initially declaring he wouldn't marry anyone under six feet tall, he realized how few and far between the pool of candidates was and lowered his standards by two inches—something he was unwilling to do with any of his other requirements.

In addition to being tall, his future wife needed to be a horse person. He felt magnanimous in the fact that she didn't have to be wealthy; lots of old horse families had maintained their lineage while losing their wealth. Times being what they were, he didn't require a dowry, although he did require patrician stock. In the United States, that limited his choices to the Kentucky area because everyone knew if you were serious about horses, you came to Kentucky. Even the queen of England bought horses from their fine state, though she didn't currently own any of the Honeywell's stock. In thinking about the queen, he decided that if he couldn't find what he was looking for in the states, Darcy would be willing to try the United Kingdom. Brits, Scots, Welsh, and even the Irish knew their horses, but they weren't necessarily tall—a quandary if there ever was one.

Having decided that he would be willing to travel out of the country in search of perfection, he found exactly what he was looking for not more than five miles from his house.

He was having dinner with his brothers, something that was becoming a rarer occurrence now that Corliss and Brent were attached. Their significant others had agreed to sacrifice their presence every Monday night so the brothers could have that night together. It was the third Monday in a row they had eaten at that particular restaurant, which was an oddity in itself. For some reason, ever since Corliss and Brent found women, all the brothers were being allowed in more and more establishments. Darcy had heard whispers about the taming effect the women were having on the men, but since he had no idea what that meant, he paid the gossip no mind.

Everett had said something particularly funny when Darcy threw back his head to laugh, and that was when he saw her. She was standing at the counter, all 5'10" of her, and she was wearing a riding habit. As if in a trance, he left his brothers and walked over to her, introduced himself, and asked her out for a date. She agreed, and Darcy had been elated. He couldn't remember the last time he had been so giddy over a woman, if he ever had.

Her name was Vivian Lawrence. When he learned she was from Virginia, he had taken a moment to mentally berate himself. Why hadn't he considered Virginia? They had a respectable horse population over there. He couldn't believe he had been willing to fly across the ocean without giving Virginia a try. Vivian's family had been breeding horses almost as long as the Honeywells, though on a much smaller scale, which was why he had never heard of her. Or maybe it was fate that had kept her name away from his ears for so long. That way, when he met her, he would know immediately that she was the one he had been searching for.

She was pretty, well bred, intelligent, and well educated. All in all, she was lovely; she was perfect; she was his dream. That was why, when his parents told him he couldn't go out with her, he hit the roof.

"What do you mean I have to cancel my date?" he roared when they asked him into the den after supper.

"We didn't say cancel, we said postpone," his mother said, her genteel tone working as an automatic reminder to lower his voice. "Your Aunt Jo has requested you, Darcy. We're very worried about her, and we want you to go check on her."

"Mom, I'll hire a private nurse. I'll do anything. But I can't go there and stay for any length of time."

His mother had remained silent, giving him "the look," the one that said she was on the verge of being disappointed with him. He and his brothers knew that look well and would do anything to make it go away. Anything but this.

"Why does she want me?" he asked.

"You know why," his father said. "Because you're an equine vet, and there's nothing she cares about more than her horses."

"She doesn't have horses," Darcy said resentfully. "She has house pets."

"Darcy," his father said in his sternest no-nonsense voice. "Jo may be eccentric, but she's my aunt, and I love her. We're her only family, and she doesn't ask much of us. In fact, this is the first time I ever remember her asking for anything. She wants you specifically, and she wants you to stay for two weeks until she's back on her feet. If you don't go, she'll work herself to death trying to oversee her herd. I will be extremely upset if that happens."

Darcy rubbed the back of his neck and sighed. "It's not that I mind helping Aunt Jo," he lied. "It's that I have a date Friday, and I'm particularly anxious about it. Can't I put off going a few days and leave on Saturday?"

His parents sat across from him, silent and stone-faced. At last his mother spoke. "I'm sure your young lady is very lovely. As such, I'm sure she'll understand a family obligation and be willing to reschedule your date."

"She lives in Virginia," he tried. "She's only here for a short time."

"Virginia isn't so far away. Spend two weeks with Aunt Jo, and you can have a week off to go to Virginia and woo this girl." This came from his father who knew exactly how to reach his middle child. Being the only equine vet in charge of such a large herd, Darcy didn't get a lot of time off.

"All right," he agreed. "I'll go to Aunt Jo's, but I am not letting one of those creatures sleep in the house with me."

"It's her house, Darcy," his mother pointed out.

"It's all of our house, and it's unsanitary. I'll look over their care, but I absolutely put my foot down at having one of those things in the house with me."

His father sighed impatiently. "Fine. I don't think she does that when the weather is warm anyway. You know they don't tolerate the cold well, but since we heated her barn I think they've been staying outside."

Darcy didn't care. He didn't care about heated barns or his aunt's stupid animals. Truth be told, he didn't care much about his aunt, either. The old girl was the toughest woman he had ever met. His father hadn't been exaggerating when he said she was eccentric. She had never married, choosing instead to devote her life to her animals. She was nothing like his mother or any of the women Darcy was used to. Instead, she was as brawny and abrupt as any man, telling anyone who would listen her opinion on life. Most of Darcy's memories of her involved working himself to death on her farm. Even though it was a tenth the size of their spread, he had somehow done more physical labor there than he ever had at home. His aunt's diehard philosophy was that physical labor kept little boys out of trouble. So every year he and his brothers had been dutifully sent to visit Aunt Jo. And every year she had almost killed them with a workload that was too heavy for most adults. Though he and his brothers considered themselves a hale and hearty, rough and tumble bunch, Aunt Jo was more than they could handle. Without exception, all of them had dreaded their annual visit to her house.

Maybe it was that same dread that made Darcy loathe to go there now. Whatever the reason, he was angry as he packed his bags and loaded them in his SUV. The drive southeast had never seemed so long, or so hilly. While his family lived in a civilized suburb outside of Lexington, his aunt lived in the middle of nowhere, surrounded by hills she liked to call mountains. People where she lived were…different. He wasn't sure how to explain them, but he and his brothers had kept to themselves when they were young, preferring their own company to the town kids whose accents were so thick they were indecipherable. It wasn't unusual to hear someone prescribe back-woods treatments for everyday maladies, such as the time he over-heard someone in town recommending to steal a washrag and bury it under a rock to get rid of warts.

Three hours later, he arrived at his aunt's farm. Technically it was his father's farm, but he let his aunt live there rent free. To her credit, she took good care of the place, doing all the manual labor and upkeep herself. And she was the uncomplaining sort. He had no doubt that if she wasn't under the weather, she never would have called to ask him for help. Perhaps the fact that she had was a sign of how sick she was.

He frowned as he wound up her long lane. What if she was truly ill? He was ill equipped to take care of an invalid old woman. Give him a sick horse, and he could work wonders, but he had no patience for sick people. He made up his mind to be solicitous and caring. Aunt Jo might truly need him. Maybe they could make a fresh start of things and have the type of nephew/aunt relationship he'd seen on television—the kind where the aunt doted on her nephew, baking him special treats and listening to his secrets. Admittedly, he was a little past the secret-sharing stage, but a thaw in their relationship would suit him fine.

His first glimpse of his aunt dispelled that notion, though. Not only did she look perfectly healthy, but she pounced on him the moment he walked in the door.

"About time you got here, Darcy. Here's a list of my animals and what needs looked at. I wrote down their food preference by animal, and also their preferred sleeping arrangements. Now, make sure and mix their food right, or they won't eat. And you have to talk to them while you're checking them over, otherwise they'll be skittish. Tomorrow you're going to have to go into town and buy some more supplies because I'm running low."

He stood in the entryway, blinking at her, waiting for her to say one word of greeting or acknowledgement about his sacrifice. He should have known better.

"Well? What are you waiting for? Scoot." She made a shooing motion with her hand, herded him toward the door, and slammed it behind him as soon as he stepped onto the porch.

CHAPTER 2

"You've got to be kidding me."

Darcy stood in the middle of his aunt's barn, surrounded by a herd of miniature horses. They were so tiny and he was so large that they seemed Lilliputian. And without exception, they were all wearing shoes. Not metal horseshoes, but actual human shoes. Or at least they looked like human shoes; in reality they were probably specialized miniature-horse shoes. They crowded around him, sniffing and pricking their ears in curiosity. Darcy had been surrounded by horses his whole life, but these weren't anything like the horses he was used to. Their size and personality were more like large dogs. When one stretched out his neck to nip the edge of Darcy's shirt, he jerked his arm back, causing the herd to scatter back to their respective stalls.

"Today I hate my life," he announced out loud. The horses poked their noses out of the stalls, creeping toward him again. This time he stood still, allowing them to sniff and nip him to their heart's content, knowing that the sooner they got it over with, the sooner they would ignore him. Or at least that was his hope. If they trailed after him like they did his Aunt Jo, he didn't know what he would do. The tallest one came up to his thigh, making him feel like Goliath. The last thing he needed was for them to take a liking to him.

A scurrying sound from outside the barn caused the horses to scatter once again. Darcy cocked his head curiously, probably resembling one of the cursed animals who also stood in the same position, staring at the door. He watched as a small child opened the door and poked his head inside, looking to and fro as if to see if the coast was clear. Somehow, he missed Darcy in his inspection. Stepping inside, he boldly began to load his arms with paraphernalia, food, horse treats, and anything else he could get his hands on. Darcy was immediately outraged; he couldn't stand thievery.

"Hey!" he yelled in his most authoritative voice. The kid dropped his booty and backed away, tripping over a metal scoop as Darcy advanced on him. Darcy reached him and grabbed him by the scruff of the neck, hauling him to his feet, which was a big mistake. The kid was as slippery as an eel. He reached around Darcy, grabbed a snow shovel, and used it to hit Darcy upside the head.

"Ouch," Darcy said. He dropped the kid and rubbed the side of his head. Instead of running away, the kid rounded on him, prepared to use the shovel again if need be. Darcy held up his hands. "Calm down, kid."

"Who are you and what are you doing here?" the boy said, only he wasn't a boy, he was a girl. From far away in the dark interior of the barn, Darcy had only been able to see a tiny form and scruffy hair. Even now, close up, it was hard to tell the difference. She had the body of a boy with the delicate features and feminine voice of a girl.

"I could ask you the same question," he said.

"But I'm the one with the shovel." She jabbed it menacingly in his direction.

He laughed and took it from her, plucking it easily from her fingers even when she struggled. Since she looked ready to flee again, he decided to tell her his name. "I'm Darcy Honeywell, and I own this property."

"I thought Jo owns this property," she said suspiciously.

"The Honeywell family owns this property. When Jo dies, it will go to me and my brothers."

"So, what, you come up here occasionally to see if she's kicked it?"

He frowned. "You're a rude kid. I have no desire for this property. I hope Jo lives a long life here because after she goes, it's only going to mean a bunch of headaches trying to sell the place." He paused, his frown deepening to a scowl. "Who are you? Why are you trying to steal things?" Her accent wasn't deep enough to make her a local.

"I'm a friend of Jo's," she said. "And I wasn't stealing anything; I've been looking after her horses since she fell ill."

"I wasn't aware my aunt had any friends," he said.

"Then you don't know her at all." She turned toward the house.

"Where are you going?" he asked, miffed over her dismissive attitude.

"To see Jo," she said.

"Jo's sick; she's not in any shape for visitors."

The girl laughed. "She'll see me."

He caught up with her in two steps and laid a hand on her shoulder to stop her. She jerked out of his grasp and rounded on him again. "What is with you? Don't you know you're not supposed to touch people without their permission?"

He held up his hands again because it had worked to subdue her the first time. "I really think you should go home now," he said in a gently authoritative tone. "It's almost suppertime, and your people will probably be worried. Maybe you can come back tomorrow after I talk to Jo about you and make sure it's okay for you to be here."

In answer, she laughed again before turning back toward the house.

Totally outraged now, Darcy said the first thing that came to mind. "Why don't you run along home to Bilbo and Frodo?"

She stopped short, spun, and faced him with her hands on her hips. "Did you call me a hobbit?"

"I guess I did," he said, trying not to sound surprised. He wasn't sure he had called a girl a name since middle school.

"You know if I'm a hobbit that makes you a troll. By the way, your barn door is open and your horses are getting out."

Growing up with four brothers made him look down at the zipper on his pants, but she pointed behind him to the barn. He turned to see all the little miniature horses making a mad dash for freedom. "Help me," he pled as he sped toward the barn.

"Hobbits don't like horses," she said unconcernedly as she turned and walked toward the house.

It took Darcy a long time to round up all the stupid animals and herd them back into the barn. He felt disloyal admitting it, but they seemed more intelligent than their full-sized cousins, outwitting him at several turns. Or maybe he was dumber here. That would explain a lot, like how he had gotten into an argument with a scruffy teenage girl and ended up calling her a hobbit. What if she was actually a dwarf or had some other growth problem? She was certainly tiny enough. He would be surprised if she cleared five feet.

He should probably apologize, but as soon as he entered the house, all his good intentions fled. It didn't take him long to realize that the raucous laughter coming from the living room was about him.

"Tell me again what he said," Jo commanded.

The girl made her voice low and spoke. "'The Honeywell family owns this property. When Jo dies, it will go to me and my brothers.'"

Jo howled with laughter, coughing midway through. "No, that part's funny, but I meant the other part."

"'Why don't you run along home to Bilbo and Frodo?'"

Darcy entered the room then and saw the girl stomping around on her toes. Apparently she was attempting to imitate him, but the expression on his face wasn't really that haughty, was it? She caught sight of him and stood to attention, giving him a brief curtsy.

"My lord," she said. "If you'll permit me some more time with your aunt, I'll make sure and empty my pockets of any pilfered silver when I leave."

Jo practically screamed with laughter, wiping her cheeks with the edge of her sleeve.

Darcy turned on his heel to go, but his aunt called him back.

"Oh, quit pouting, Darcy, and come in here. He's always been the stuffiest one," she added in an aside that he heard as clearly as if she had said it to him. He reentered the room and stood sullenly awaiting her next instruction. "This is my good friend Genevieve Porter. *Dr. Genevieve Porter, that is.*"

Darcy stared at the tiny creature in astonishment. "You're a doctor?" How was that possible? She didn't look any older than sixteen.

"I'm a psychologist. Though I should tell you I'm a family therapist. Narcissism on such a grand scale is beyond my ability." She extended her hand in a friendly manner as if she hadn't insulted him. Jo chuckled again.

"Gen, you've already met Darcy. He's my third nephew, but if he doesn't shape up, I can switch him for one of his brothers." Jo scowled at him as if his being there was a grand privilege she might revoke at any moment.

"Mr. Honeywell," Genevieve said demurely, curtsying again.

"It's Dr. Honeywell, actually," Darcy said, peeved beyond all rationality by the two irritating women who had decided to gang up on him.

Genevieve smiled in a way that let him know she was making fun of him in her head. "Is that what you would like me to call you?"

He took a deep breath and held it a few beats, releasing it slowly through his teeth. "You can call me Darcy." He hoped this would be the last time he saw her for the remainder of his stay, but his aunt soon dispelled that notion.

"Might as well learn to unbend and make friends with her, Darce. You'll see her every day."

He hated to be called Darce, which he was sure his aunt knew very well.

"Yeah, Darce," Genevieve added with a mischievous smile.

He ignored her and addressed his aunt. "Why does she come here every day?"

"To see to the horses," his aunt said.

"I thought that's what I'm here for," he said. He could feel his patience reaching its limit, and he fought for control.

"You're here to see to their physical wellbeing. Genevieve oversees their emotional wellbeing."

He quirked an eyebrow at Genevieve. "You provide therapy for the horses?"

"Not the horses," she said.

He looked at his aunt. She held up her hands. "Don't look at me. I don't need therapy."

"I'm here for you," Genevieve said sincerely to Darcy. "This is an intervention."

"What?" he said, his head swiveling between them.

"That was a joke. Don't worry, Dr. Honeywell. You'll catch on to the way we do things here soon enough." She leaned down to kiss Jo on her cheek. "I'll see you tomorrow, lovely lady. Call and let me know if there's anything I can bring you."

"I'll do that, sweetheart. You take care."

Darcy had to fight the urge to do a double take. He had never heard his aunt call anyone "sweetheart" in his life. He hadn't known the word was in her vocabulary.

"Genevieve brought supper," Jo announced, sounding cheerful for the first time in his life. Her usual tone was gruff. What power did this Genevieve person wield over his aunt? How had she been able to charm her way into the old lady's good graces so completely? Did she have designs on Jo's wealth? Granted, Jo didn't have as much as his portion of the family did, but she had no children. Upon her death, everything would go to him and his brothers unless she willed it otherwise. He didn't want or need her money, but he also didn't want to see her fritter it away on some hapless woman who was as eccentric as she was. What if this Genevieve person had wormed her way to her aunt's heart for some sort of ill purpose? What if she wasn't a doctor at all? How could she be? She looked half his age, and he was only thirty.

"How old is she?"

"Who?" his aunt asked as she set out containers of food and dishes.

"The girl, Genevieve."

"The *woman* is somewhere in her mid twenties."

"And she has her doctorate already?"

"Gen's a marvel," Jo said sincerely. "She graduated high school at fourteen." She paused in filling her plate to scowl at Darcy. "Don't you give her a hard time, you hear? She's been through enough. You be nice to her."

When am I ever not nice? he started to ask, but held himself back, reviewing the day in his head. Maybe he hadn't been so nice, but tomorrow he would do better. With that thought in mind, he listened patiently as his aunt detailed the medical history for each of her thirty horses.

CHAPTER 3

The next day, Darcy felt like he was holding his breath, waiting for the other shoe to drop. He was as skittish as a newborn foal, jumping at every sound, waiting for the tiny Genevieve creature to make an appearance. When she did, he almost missed it because he was in the barn, giving each horse a complete physical, per his aunt's instructions. He found himself warming to the little pests, but he assured himself it was simply because, as a veterinarian, he was supposed to love all animals.

As the day wore on, he began to talk to the animals, telling them about his day and about Vivian, his new love interest. Was it his imagination, or did they look at him sympathetically, as if they understood what he was saying.

"Talking to the animals, Dr. Doolittle?"

Darcy jumped and practically fell off his stool when Genevieve sneaked up on him. She ignored his discomfiture, focusing instead on the horses.

"Hey, old girl," she said, giving the horse a gentle scratch on her neck. The horse squinted happily and leaned into her hand. "Did you know miniature horses could live to be thirty five years old?"

"Really?" he drawled. "I guess all those years of veterinary school were for nothing when I could as easily have gotten my information from a random psychologist."

"Whoa, dial down the rage there, doctor. I was merely making conversation. And I also came to tell you dinner is ready." She turned and went back the way she came.

He pulled off his gloves and tossed them angrily into the trash can. What was it about the woman that drove him crazy? He wasn't usually so snappish. In fact, he was known for his friendliness and flirtatiousness. Maybe that was the problem. Maybe because he had no desire to flirt with her he wasn't sure what to do with her. He tried to muster an ounce of flirtatious energy for her and couldn't. She wasn't attractive. Shorter than him by a couple of feet, she was wiry with unstylish, choppy hair, a pale complexion and ill-fitting boyish clothes. For some reason, her appearance irritated him as much as her personality. Couldn't she at least try to look pretty? Couldn't she try to look like a woman instead of a fifteen-year-old boy?

He was still in a roaring bad mood when he entered the house, although the scent of food worked a little to calm him. By the mess on the counter, he understood that Genevieve had been there for some time cooking while he was in the barn.

"You really shouldn't be spoiling us this way, Gen," Jo said, though she sounded delighted by Genevieve's efforts.

"Of course I should," Genevieve answered. "You would do the same for me, and in fact, you did." The two women shared a smile while Darcy watched with halfhearted interest.

His first bite of food caught his interest and held it, which was good because his aunt and Genevieve began talking about people he didn't know, remaining on the subject for some time. He had seconds and then thirds before realizing that, not only had he rudely taken all the food, but he hadn't said a word or added to the conversation.

When he looked up, Genevieve was watching him, her eyes sparkling with amusement. Her eyes might be her one nice feature. They were a dark shade of blue with flecks of gold and green around the irises. Too bad the rest of her was so lackluster.

"Supper is delicious," he said.

Her smile widened. "Thank you. I'm glad you approve. I'm sorry I've been so rude, chatting away about people you've never met. Tell me about you. What makes Dr. Honeywell tick?"

"Is this a therapy session?"

"Do you need it to be?" She picked at her fried chicken, nibbling a small bite. He realized she was still working on the same small piece she had started with and frowned.

"Don't you eat?"

"When I can. Jo tells me you're from a large family. That must have been fun."

"You don't have siblings?"

She shook her head, her amusement deepening. "You're really good at dodging questions. Do I make you nervous?"

He laughed, but he *was* uncomfortable with the questions. Like any good southern male, he was suspicious of therapy and therapists. He was afraid she was secretly analyzing him, trying to find crazy where no crazy existed.

As if guessing his thoughts, she held up her right hand like she was taking an oath. "I promise anything you tell me is strictly off the record. I'll only analyze you if you pay me to do so. I'm money-grubbing that way." Beside her, Jo chuckled.

Darcy's brow puckered, not sure if she was kidding. Was she after money? How had she swayed his crusty aunt? Granted, it was nice that she brought food, but food was a small price to pay for lifelong financial comfort.

"Okay, then," Genevieve drawled. "Conversation isn't your strong suit. That's okay; I prefer the strong, silent type." She stood and began clearing the table.

"Sit, honey, I'll get those," Jo said. She tried to stand, but Genevieve put a hand on her shoulder and pushed her back down.

"You'll do no such thing, Josephine. Don't make me tie you to that chair. You sit there and keep me company. Or, better yet, go watch your program. I'll join you when I'm finished."

Unbelievably, his aunt complied. Darcy had a difficult time hiding his astonishment. "How did you do that?" he whispered.

She paused halfway to the sink and looked at him. "Do what?"

"Get my aunt to do what you told her. No one else in my family has ever been able to accomplish that."

Genevieve shrugged. "I love her, and she knows it. I want what's best for her. My motives are pure."

He wasn't sure if she was trying to reassure him on a grander scale about her intentions concerning his aunt. She seemed to be able to read his mind, a fact which he found most disconcerting. "We all care about Aunt Jo, but none of us has ever found her pliable. Even my dad who was originally her only nephew before any of us came along."

"I'm not sure you want to hear my opinion on the matter, so I'll wisely keep silent," Genevieve said, filling the sink with soapy water.

Darcy stood and began carrying dishes to the sink for her. "Let's hear it," he said tightly, not sure he wanted to hear her opinion, either.

"Your family sees Jo as an eccentric liability, a doddering old lady who wiles away lonely hours on her pets. I see Jo as vital to this community and to my personal wellbeing. She's the closest thing I have to family, and she's the most caring and genuine individual I know. I suppose you could say she's my mentor."

"Look," Darcy spoke patiently. "I don't know you, and I know that my aunt is a good woman who is very upright, but it concerns me to hear you say she's your mentor. She's…" He trailed off, searching for the right word.

Genevieve paused, anger flashing in her face. "She's what? Eccentric? I already knew that, and I don't believe there's anything wrong with it."

"I was going to say lonely," he said quietly. "We're her only family and we're three hours away. We're lucky if we see her once a year, and even then she doesn't really open up to us."

"I'm her family," Genevieve insisted. "And so are the people in this community. We all love Jo, and she loves us. We take care of her, and she takes care of us. There's a vast difference in being alone and being lonely."

"If you say so," he said, clearly unconvinced.

She slammed a pot on the counter, and he jumped. "Look, let's get one thing straight between us. I don't care if your high and mighty bombastic attitude extends to me because I'm a strong woman, and I can handle you. But you leave Jo alone. She's the kindest, gentlest, most generous and giving person I've ever met, and she doesn't need you coming in here trying to run her life for her."

He quirked an eyebrow at her. "And you have a big stake in her generosity, is that it?"

"Yes, I do," she said easily, returning to her dishes.

He was rigid with anger over her admission that she was after Jo's money. "I don't know what you've done to trick my aunt into giving you her money, but I'm going to speak to my lawyer about it and make sure you don't get a dime you don't deserve."

To his further annoyance, she gave him the amused smile once more. "You do that," she said. "It would be nice to have all the legalities tied up." She finished the dishes, drained the sink, and dried her hands on the dishtowel he was holding. He had intended to dry for her, but became so caught up in their conversation that he had simply stood still, staring. "You make a handy towel rack," she added, giving his chest an ingratiating pat.

She meandered into the living room where he heard female chatter and the sound of laughter. By the time he dried the dishes and put them away, she was gone and Jo was asleep on the couch, a blanket tucked neatly around her. He had never seen his aunt asleep. Despite the fact that she was eighty, she had never been one of those old women who fell asleep in her chair. The sight disturbed him. Maybe he and his aunt weren't best friends, but he counted on her to be the same steady presence she had always been. He hated the thought of her getting old and frail.

On the one hand, he was glad she had someone nearby to take care of her. Genevieve certainly seemed sincere in her affections. She had brought food the last two nights, taken care of the horses for who knew how long, and also forced his aunt to rest—an amazing feat in and of itself. But he was still disturbed when he thought of her as taking advantage of his aunt's largess. Was she after the money? He made a mental note to talk to his lawyer, who also happened to be his oldest brother, Brent. Clearly they needed to take more of an interest in their aunt's affairs and make sure she was protected from anyone who might prey on her old maid status.

After peeking once more at his sleeping aunt, he picked up the remote control and turned the channel to a baseball game.

"I was watching that," his aunt snapped, startling him so badly he almost dropped the remote. He returned the channel to her show and a minute later listened to her soft snores. He sighed, closing his eyes and resting his head against the back of the chair. It was going to be a long two weeks, indeed.

CHAPTER 4

The next morning Darcy rose early to finish his examination of the horses. But even though it was barely past sunrise, Genevieve was already in the barn, wearing tall boots, overalls that looked fit for a child, and a knit skull cap. She sang softly to herself as she mucked out the stalls and refilled them with fresh straw. If he wasn't so unsure of her and so annoyed with her, he might have smiled at the sight.

"I thought I'm supposed to do that," he said.

She jumped slightly and spun to look at him with a sheepish smile. "This is my form of therapy."

"Mucking stalls?" he asked incredulously.

"Cleaning. Replacing old straw with new. Giving the horses a little bit of pleasure. I like to see how excited they get when the new straw goes in their stalls."

Weird. "I have to tell you that I grew up on a farm, and I have never heard a woman say she enjoyed mucking stalls."

"Maybe you've never met the right type of woman," she suggested. Though she had said it flippantly, he was suddenly suspicious of her. Was that what this was about? Did she have a crush on him?

"I should tell you that I'm seeing someone," he said.

She laughed out loud and set the shovel aside, shaking her head. "Dr. Honeywell, you make me laugh. But since you brought it up, I'll let you know where I stand on the matter of romance with you." She peeled off her gloves and set them aside, and then she advanced on him. He would have backed up a step, but she was so tiny, he would feel ridiculous running away from her. She grabbed a chair and dragged it along with her, positioning the chair between them.

"If I were of a mind to pursue you, I wouldn't do it wearing old overalls, a skull cap, and no makeup." She stood on the chair so they were eye level. Her eyes were once again brimming with amusement and, if it hadn't been at his expense, he might have smiled with her. "I would wear a dress, the slinky black one that shows off my curves. I would style my hair, or what's left of it." She frowned slightly and self-consciously touched her hair. "I would wear makeup and jewelry and some intoxicating scent, one whiff of which would make you crazy with longing. Then I would climb on a chair, like this. I would rest my hands on your shoulders like so," she placed her palms gently on his shoulders. "Then I would lean in and whisper something alluring." She leaned so close that her lips brushed his ear, and then she whispered. "If you were the last giant on earth, I wouldn't touch you with a ten foot pole, you overbearing, cocky, cynical cretin."

Taken unaware by her display and her proximity, Darcy was momentarily stunned, so her words didn't register until after she hopped down from the chair and donned her gloves again. Then he leaned one shoulder against a pole and crossed his arms. He had to remind himself that she meant nothing to him; her words didn't bother him. But, still, he felt bad that he had given her such a bad impression.

"I'm none of those things you said," he commented, trying hard to keep his voice casual.

"If I were of a mind to, I would say that actions speak louder than words. But since that might be rude, I won't say it," she said, focusing on her task without even looking at him.

He had the sudden desire to pick her up and make her look at him when she talked to him. What was it about this woman that made him act like a fifteen-year-old again? Where were all his smooth moves and honeyed words? It wasn't as if he didn't have experience with women. The problem, he realized, was that he had experience with normal women. Or maybe the problem was hers. He would guess it was a cold, hard fact that she had never dated before. Hadn't she admitted as much when she declared she would wind up alone like Jo? Maybe he should take her on as his project, sort of like a *My Fair Lady* type of thing. He could teach her how to talk to men, how to dress appropriately and look better. But as he studied her he had no idea how to make the suggestion. She would no doubt laugh at him again. He wasn't sure his ego could take any more battering from her.

They worked in silence as he finished his examinations. As he reached the last horse in the stall, his interested, "Hmm," drew her attention.

"What is it?' she asked, dropping the shovel to move closer. "Is there something wrong with Lou? We've been worried about her because she hasn't been acting right."

"There's nothing wrong with her that having her foal won't cure," he said.

Her mouth dropped as she looked at the little horse. "Lou? But she's twenty if she's a day, and she's never foaled before. We thought she couldn't." She reached out to pat the horse's neck. "Lou, you old dog, you."

He laughed, the first time he had done so in her presence. She turned to him with a warm smile.

"I guess this means there's hope for the rest of us," she said, giving him a wink before she turned to walk away. "I'm going to check on Jo before I leave. Come inside and I'll make you some lunch."

He turned to the horse with a smile. "You old dog, you," he repeated, laughing again. Genevieve was definitely an original. If they hadn't gotten off on the wrong foot, they would probably be friends. He imagined her meeting his brothers and laughed again. Genevieve plus the five Honeywells was a match made in heaven—he smiled, thinking of the mischief they could get into together.

He was still smiling when he entered the house. Genevieve had assembled sandwiches for lunch that looked normal, but tasted better than any he had ever had. "Where did you learn to cook?" he asked.

"Culinary school," she said.

He froze, his sandwich halfway to his mouth. "You got a doctorate and went to culinary school?"

"I needed something to do in my spare time," she said. "I don't do well with down time." Once again she barely ate enough to keep a bird alive, though that might have been because she was buzzing around making sure he and Jo ate and had refills on their tea. Finally he took the pitcher from her and pushed her into her chair.

"Sit. Eat," he commanded. "I'll pour the dang tea."

"Darcy," his aunt snapped. "Watch your language or I'll make you paint the fence."

"Yes, ma'am," he said dutifully, giving Genevieve a conspiratorial smile when his aunt returned her attention to her food.

"Gen tells me Lou is going to foal," his aunt said when he finished pouring the tea and sat down.

"Any day now, I think," he said.

She bit her lip worriedly. "Do you think she'll be okay? She's been with me since she was a foal herself, and she's no spring chicken."

"I'll think she'll be fine," he said reassuringly. "I'll keep a close eye on her. What's the point of having a nephew who's a vet if he can't keep your horses alive?"

His aunt smiled a sweet smile she had never before bestowed on him. "Why don't you two go into town today and buy some more supplies?" she suggested.

An awkward silence descended over the table, but his aunt took no notice as she continued.

"Gen can show you where to go and what to get, and you can do all the heavy lifting." She paused and looked at Genevieve. "You don't have anything going on this afternoon, do you, honey?"

"No, I don't have anything going on."

Darcy noted her tone was reluctant, and he also noted that his aunt didn't check with him to see if he had anything going on. Jo nodded in satisfaction, smiling again. "Good then, it's settled."

"Why don't you take a little siesta while we're gone, Jo?" Genevieve suggested. "You're looking a little peaked."

"Maybe I will," Jo easily acquiesced. She shoved off from the table and shuffled to the living room, leaving silence in her wake. Genevieve cleared her throat and stood to clear the table. Darcy, quicker on the draw this time, stood to help. Together they had the kitchen cleaned in a few minutes, and then it was time to go.

"We can take my car," Darcy said. He imagined her trying to see over the dashboard of a vehicle and shuddered. No, thank you, not on these twisty, hilly roads.

"Okay," she said, laughing quietly to herself.

"Why is that funny?" he asked. He was very tired of feeling like he was the butt of an inside joke with her.

"I was trying to picture you on the handlebars of my bike. Your car is a better option unless it's a unicycle."

"You ride your bike here?" he asked, aghast.

"It's not so far," she said.

He had no idea if that was true because he had no idea where she lived. "Yes, but these roads are…"

"A good workout," she provided. "A little exercise never hurt anyone."

"But being hit by a car might. Riding a bike on these roads is like suicide."

"Only if another car actually comes along, which one rarely does. And the locals know to look out for me. Who else but locals ever come out here?"

They reached his SUV, but he felt reluctant to let the topic drop. She was a grown woman, mostly, and he didn't much care for her. Why then should it bother him that she did something as crazy as ride her bicycle? He intended to help her into the tall SUV, but by the time he reached her, she had vaulted inside and was clicking her seatbelt. He bypassed her side and climbed behind the steering wheel.

"This is a fancy car," she commented, running her finger over the leather seat beside her. "Do you mind if I ask a rude question?"

"If I say no, will it stop you from asking?"

She smiled. "Probably not."

"Then fire away."

"Where does the Honeywell fortune come from?"

He frowned, not because he didn't want to answer, but because he wanted to know why it mattered to her. She didn't dress well, didn't have a car, and was mysteriously attached to his elderly aunt. "Horses," he said at last. "The Honeywells have bred horses for generations. Fine, expensive horses fit for royalty or those who are able to afford them. Since its founding, a large percentage of our horses have been in the derby. A handful has won."

"The derby?" she repeated, looking duly impressed. "Have you ever been?"

He smiled at her childlike enthusiasm. "Lots of times."

"I'm not so much into material things, but going to the derby has been a long-held dream of mine ever since I was a little girl and watched it with my grandpa on television." She paused, looking mildly embarrassed. "Sorry, I'm rambling."

Strangely, he didn't mind. He tried to remember the last time he was around someone who was so very *alive*. Genevieve seemingly took joy in everything, from the grandeur of the Kentucky derby to the undignified task of mucking stalls. He almost found himself offering to take her next time. Was he losing his grip on reality? He didn't know this girl from Eve, and yet he almost asked her to *the* social event of the year. With any luck, he would be attending the derby with Vivian. Thoughts of Vivian occupied him for so long that they were in town before he knew it. He felt bad about the lack of conversation in the car, but Genevieve didn't seem to mind. Or, if she did, she didn't lose her smile. She bounded from the car, waiting impatiently for him so they could walk to the feed store together.

At least he thought she was waiting for him. She might have been waiting to receive her admirers because seemingly from nowhere people began to emerge and assemble, as if she were a celebrity and they were her adoring fan club. Everyone had a word or question for Genevieve, and she had a hug or reply for each of them. After satisfying themselves that Genevieve was truly in their presence, they turned suspicious frowns on him, which was surprising. He had always thought the people in this town strange but friendly.

Genevieve jerked her thumb in his direction. "Jo's nephew."

The worried frowns went away, only to be replaced by welcoming smiles. "We thought you were Gen's new beaux," one lady explained. Darcy almost laughed before realizing she was serious. Did these people really think he would be with Genevieve? And, if so, was that something they wouldn't approve of? The mystery was deepening, and Darcy was feeling more annoyed. He stood back while the assembled crowd asked about Jo and offered their services to her, through Genevieve of course.

"What do you need us to do for her, Gen?" a middle-aged man asked.

"Her nephew is staying here for the time being, but after he leaves, there's going to be a lot to do, Tom. Thank you for asking. I think y'all know me well enough to know that I'll have no trouble asking for your help when the need arises."

"Yeah, you'll ask for help for *Jo*," another person said. Darcy didn't understand his accusing attitude. Did the man also think Genevieve was using Jo for her money?

Genevieve laughed. "That's right; I'll ask for help for Jo. I think what she needs now is a little rest and some TLC, both of which Mr. Honeywell can provide. Speaking of which, I'd better get Jo's purchases and get him home. Lou is going to foal soon."

There were murmurs and exclamations among the small crowd. Genevieve surprised Darcy by reaching for his hand and tugging him toward the store.

"They really care that a horse is going to foal?" Darcy asked as soon as they were away from the crowd.

"Of course not. But they care about Jo, and Jo cares about her horses. They're excited for her," Genevieve answered. She dropped his hand when they entered the store, and the round of celebrity greetings started all over again. One man in particular seemed a little too happy to see her.

"Gen!" he exclaimed. Rushing around from behind the counter, he swept her up in a hug and twirled her in a circle. "I didn't know you were coming into town today. Isn't it Wednesday?"

"Nope, it's Tuesday." She returned the man's hug, squeezing him tightly around the neck. He reluctantly set her down and stood back with a smile. "You're looking good, Gen."

Genevieve laughed as if he had said something really funny. She reached up to pat his cheek. "Aren't you the sweetest liar, Luke?"

"I'm serious," the man insisted, though Darcy thought he looked more like a boy. Was it something in the water here that kept everyone looking like adolescents? He cleared his throat and stepped forward. The man, Luke, dropped Genevieve's hand and gave Darcy the narrow-eyed look he was becoming used to.

"Who's this?" Luke asked.

"Jo's nephew," Genevieve explained. She reached in her pocket and pulled out a folded piece of paper. "Here's her list."

Luke took the list and looked over it. "Keep me company while I gather these things, sweetheart," he said. Folding the note, he tucked it into his pocket and lifted Genevieve up onto the counter. She crossed her legs Indian style and began chattering to Luke as he loaded the large feed bags onto a cart.

Darcy remained in the middle of the store, feeling helpless and out of sorts. He had never before realized how much being a Honeywell meant to him. In his small town of Silver Springs, they were practically royalty, known by reputation as well as appearance. Even in Lexington, their name carried weight. But here, in the boonies, the only Honeywell of importance was his odd aunt. He didn't enjoy the discombobulating feeling of being without his brothers. Without them and without his family name, who was he?

Genevieve paused in her conversation to look over her shoulder and smile at him. Motioning him forward, she returned to her conversation with Luke. Darcy came to stand beside her, realizing as he did so that she was asking gentle questions about Luke and his family. Luke chatted happily as he loaded the cart, filling Genevieve in on the mundane details of his life. But Genevieve didn't look bored.

She looked like the tale of his grandmother's latest ailment was the most fascinating news she had ever heard.

"I'm so sorry to hear she's been under the weather," she said sympathetically. "Please tell her I hope she's better soon."

"I'll do that, sweetheart, but she probably would love a visit from you when you get the chance. She says you're a little ray of sunshine, lighting up a room."

"That's sweet," Genevieve said, smiling. "Tell her I'll be around as soon as I'm sure Jo is safely on the mend."

Darcy frowned. Did Genevieve prey on all the elderly in the town? Was this Luke person's grandmother wealthy, too? Somehow he doubted it, but why else would Genevieve think it her duty to visit all the sick old people in the community? Could she really be as caring and selfless as she seemed? Was he, as she had accused, simply being cynical?

Luke finished loading the bags of feed onto the push cart and turned to Genevieve with a smile. "Please don't tell me you brought your bike, Gen," he said.

Genevieve laughed and hopped off the counter top. "That would be a sight, now wouldn't it? Doctor Honeywell gave me a ride," she said, beaming an impish smile at Darcy.

"Doctor?" Luke repeated with a whistle. "Now that's impressive."

"Hey, I'm a doctor," Genevieve protested. "And you've never said I'm impressive."

"You're impressive for better, different reasons," Luke said, grinning.

They reached the SUV and Darcy shooed him aside. "I can get these. You can run along inside to your other customers."

"But they're fifty pound bags," Luke protested.

Darcy gave him a disbelieving look. Did the guy think he was a cream puff? He was a good ten inches taller than Luke, with broader shoulders and, he would wager, more developed muscles. As if to prove his unspoken point, he bent and lifted all the bags at once, not realizing his mistake until he tossed them onto his shoulder. Two hundred pounds of feed knocked against his head, bumping it out of alignment. He tossed them into the truck, tried to bend his head back into place, and found that he couldn't.

"I'll wait in the truck," he said in order to cover the now awkward, corkscrew configuration of his neck.

Genevieve said goodbye to Luke—with a hug, Darcy noted—and joined him in the truck. "We only have one more stop," she said. He suppressed a groan as he pulled into the grocery store. "Would you care to wait here?" she asked.

"If you're sure you don't need me," Darcy replied with forced casualness. In reality, his neck was killing him and he was developing a headache.

"I'll only be a tick," she replied, dashing out of the car with a springy jump. As soon as she was gone, Darcy tried manipulating his sore neck back into proper alignment, but he couldn't, and he was in agony.

True to her word, Genevieve returned in short order, and she was loaded down with bags. Darcy stumbled out of the car to help her, but by the time he reached her, she had already loaded them into the back. She looked up at him, tilting her head.

"You okay?" she asked.

"Sure thing," he lied, trying not to grimace. This time he had ample opportunity to help her into the vehicle, but, tiny as she was, he was afraid to lift her for fear of doing further damage to himself. Instead he opened her door and watched while she lightly sprang into the seat, eyeing him warily all the while.

He climbed slowly into his seat like an old man. His ears were ringing and he was trying to think where the nearest chiropractor might be. Surely there wasn't one in this tiny town. Would he have to drive all the way back to Lexington?

They were silent on the drive back to his aunt's farm. He turned to open his door but looked at Genevieve in surprise when she laid her hand on his forearm.

"Be honest with me," she said. "Did you hurt your neck at the feed store?"

He couldn't lie to a direct question but, oh, how he wanted to. "It's nothing," he said dismissively. He reached for his door again and, once again, she held him back.

"This goes against my better judgment, but I'm going to help you. Face the door." She sat up on her knees and, before he could protest, her hands were on his neck, lifting it until he felt like it was going to pop off his head. With her right hand she gently kneaded whatever was out of whack back into place. There was an almost audible "POP" and, like magic, Darcy's headache went away as his range of motion returned to normal. He closed his eyes while she gently massaged his neck for another minute, making sure everything was back in alignment.

"There you go," she said.

He inhaled deeply and let it out slowly. The physical relief was so intense, he felt like laughing. "Don't tell me you're a chiropractor, too."

"Nah," she said. "I dated one for a while. He taught me some moves. Not those type of moves," she said when Darcy's eyebrows rose in surprise. To his amusement, she was blushing.

He was finally able to help her carry the bags of groceries, and when he did, he frowned. "What's all this stuff for?" By his count, he saw three loaves of bread, several containers of cheese spread, carrots, dip, and lemonade mix, all in mass quantities. "Surely this isn't all for Jo, is it?"

Either Genevieve didn't hear the question, or she pretended not to because she didn't answer. Instead, she bypassed him and went to check on Jo who was sitting in front of the television, watching her programs. When she returned to the kitchen, Darcy was leaning against the counter, still awaiting her reply.

"Is she having a party?"

"You'll have to ask her about that," Genevieve said. "I'm going to make supper now."

"You don't have to do this; you don't have to keep feeding us."

"Are you going to cook?" she asked with a smile.

"Not unless I want to kill Jo and myself. But I could hire someone."

She waved her hand dismissively. "Why do that when I'm here every day anyway? Unless you'd rather I didn't." She paused and looked up at him, sounding uncertain for the first time since he met her.

"Where else am I going to get a trained chef for free?" he asked, returning her smile.

"I wouldn't exactly say I'm free," she said, resuming her preparations.

His smile slipped slightly. What did that mean?

She turned her head up again. "Want to be my sous chef?"

"I have no idea how," he said, though he found that he wanted to. She made kitchen work look like fun.

"You can wield the knife. That's a manly sort of task."

She gave him a cutting board, knife, and vegetables. He began arduously slicing, but she didn't chide him for taking so long. At least, not until he sliced his finger. He was content to wrap it and keep going, but she clucked her tongue at him and took his hand in hers, inspecting the cut.

"This needs a bandage," she said.

"It's fine," he assured her.

"Blood in food is not fine," she said. She sifted through the catchall drawer until she located the box of bandages and applied one to his wound. "This isn't your day, huh?" she asked as she smoothed her finger over the wound, sealing the bandage.

"It hasn't been my day since I arrived here," he said.

Her answering smile was sympathetic and they finished their dinner prep in silence.

CHAPTER 5

*A*fter supper, Darcy insisted on driving Genevieve home. The thought of her riding her bike on the winding roads during the daytime was bad enough, but the thought of her on them at night was nightmare inducing.

"You really don't have to do this," she said as she loaded her bike in the back of his SUV. He had opened the trunk, intending to stow the bike for her, but when he turned around, she was already stuffing it inside. Then she quickly darted to the passenger door and vaulted into the seat before he could offer assistance there, either.

With a sigh, he closed the trunk and walked to his side of the vehicle, jumping inside. The only conversation during the ride consisted of her giving directions to her house. It was a small little place at the edge of town, but he supposed someone as tiny as she didn't need a large space.

"Don't ride your bike tomorrow," he said before she could spring from the car. "I'll pick you up."

"Actually, I'm driving tomorrow, but thank you for the offer. I really don't mind riding my bike."

"Nonetheless, I would prefer it if you didn't ride your bike again while I'm here. If you need a ride, you can call me."

"I don't have a phone," she said.

"Then we'll work something out," he said.

She smiled. "You're a very manly sort of man," she commented.

He frowned. "When you say that, it sounds like a bad thing."

"No, it's not, especially because nothing compels me to follow your instructions. I can simply listen and pretend it's charming." She reached for her door, but he stopped her again.

"While we're on the subject, I should also tell you that it's generally considered chivalrous for the man to get your door and help you down. Stay there."

She gave him her usual amused expression, but did as he commanded, remaining as still as a stone until he opened the door, reached for her, and lifted her down.

"Well that was very nice, but also very unnecessary," she said as they walked up her short sidewalk. "What's the point of doing something I can so easily do myself?"

"It's supposed to make you feel…cared for, I suppose."

She leaned against the doorframe, thinking. "Hmm, I can see your point, and I think other women might like that sort of thing, but it's lost on me. I like doing things for myself. Now, if you could do something I couldn't do, well, that would be impressive."

"Is there anything you can't do?" he asked sincerely. One thing he could say about her was that she was certainly capable.

"I can't reach things on the top shelf without standing on the counter."

"Basically you're saying that you want someone who can take the place of a footstool," he said.

"A footstool who's a good kisser," she said, surprising him so much he laughed out loud. She smiled up at him. "See you tomorrow, Doc. Thanks again for the ride." She walked inside and closed the door in his face, making Darcy realize he had actually been expecting an invitation inside.

T he next day, Darcy beat Genevieve to the barn and realized he missed her odd little presence. With a start, he comprehended that she was starting to charm her way into his affections and resolved to steel himself against her, at least until he had her figured out. She seemed warm and sincere, and she was certainly a cheerful ray of sunshine, but he felt like there was something he was missing, and it made him suspicious. Though, the more he thought about it, the more he found himself wanting to clear his suspicions and give her approval. What if she was one of those rare individuals who was purely good?

Later that morning, the sound of an engine alerted him to the fact that someone had arrived, most likely Genevieve. But when he poked his head out of the barn to check, he saw a large conversion van. He didn't see anyone behind the wheel, but Genevieve hopped out of the driver's side. He smiled—he really *couldn't* see her behind the wheel when she drove.

She began opening doors and children began to descend from the vehicle, chattering excitedly and dashing toward the barn, toward him. He stood rooted to the spot, trying to figure out what was going on. Once all the kids were emptied from the van, Genevieve turned and began running after them, laughing as excitedly as they did. The entire group, Genevieve and a dozen kids, came to a screeching halt in front of Darcy, and all of them looked up at him with a pensive, worried expression.

Darcy skimmed the children and saw at a glance that they had one thing in common. They were all very ill. Small, frail, pale, and, in many cases, bald, they stared up at him with rounded, frightened eyes that tugged at his heart, rendering him speechless. His eyes sought Genevieve. Today she was dressed professionally with khaki pants and a blue sweater. He wondered if she wore makeup because today her face had more color, her eyes were brighter blue, and for the first time he saw a dimple in her right cheek. On her head, she wore a dew rag, but Darcy wondered if she did it as a way of relating to the children, many of whom were wearing the same sort of thing.

"Guys, this is Dr. Honeywell," Genevieve said. The kids looked even more worried. He guessed they were probably leery of all doctors now. "He's a special doctor for the animals," she hastened to explain.

"Are they sick?" one little boy asked worriedly.

"No, of course not," Genevieve explained. "Dr. Honeywell takes such good care of them, they don't get sick. And I'll tell you a secret, but you have to promise not to let him know I told you." They stared at her excitedly as she lowered her voice to a conspiratorial whisper and put her hand over her mouth, shielding it from Darcy's view. "He talks to the animals." The kids giggled and turned their smiling gazes on Darcy.

"Do the animals talk back?" one little girl asked.

"Why don't you ask him," Genevieve suggested.

"Do the animals talk to you, Dr.?" the little girl said, a frightened quaver in her voice. Darcy thought his large size might be intimidating them. He knelt and, on his knees, he was eye level with most of them.

"Well, they're a little shy," he said. "But one in particular has started to trust me. Yesterday he told me a secret." He looked around at a tiny horse, the one who most often followed him around the barn as he worked. "Do you want to know his secret?"

They nodded their assent, and he continued.

"He has a crush on someone in this very room."

They gasped and giggled. "Who is it?" the little girl asked.

"Guess," Darcy replied with a significant look at Genevieve.

"It's Genevieve," the kids chorused, looking up at their leader with adoration. "Is it Genevieve?" one of them asked Darcy.

"I can't say for certain and give away his secret. How would he ever trust me again?" Behind his back, he motioned, calling for the horse. As if on cue, the horse trotted up and nuzzled Genevieve while the children squealed with laughter. Genevieve played her part well, scratching the horse behind the ear so he closed his eyes and leaned into her touch. After fawning over the horse for a few minutes, she turned to the kids and clapped her hands.

"All right, guys, let's get started. Go choose your horse," she announced. Darcy watched as the kids ran to a stall, standing quietly in front until Genevieve gave further instructions. "All right, you remember what to do," she encouraged. "Be slow and gentle."

Darcy crossed his arms, leaned against a beam and watched as the smiling kids opened the stalls and began to bridle the horses. Someone had taught them well. He presumed it had been his aunt Jo because they performed the routine in the same way she did. He watched intently to make sure none of the kids accidentally bumped the horses' lips, causing them to throw their heads, but they were all slow and gentle, as Genevieve had commanded. And in response the horses stood perfectly still, patiently allowing the kids to work.

Darcy hated to admit it, but he thought these horses might have better temperaments than the horses his family raised, and previously he had thought his horses the best behaved creatures he had ever seen. But the mini horses seemed to have a sixth sense about the kids, standing stock still while they were bridled and then lovingly nudging the kids, causing them to giggle. As soon as the horses were bridled, the children led them outside and began walking them, talking to them as they went. The snippets of their conversation as they passed by Darcy made him smile.

With all of his patients out of the barn, save one, he checked on the little mare that was getting ready to foal. She showed no signs of labor, but she was close. He gave her a gentle pat and she looked up at him with baleful eyes.

"I know you're uncomfortable, old girl," he said. "A little while longer and it will all be over."

"You really do talk to the horses," a little voice murmured. Darcy turned to see a little girl standing at the entrance of the barn, staring at him.

"I really do," he assured her. They shared a smile and she skipped back to her friends while Darcy's heart turned over. She was so fragile it seemed a stiff wind could break her; every blue vein was visible through her translucent skin. How had his aunt come to be involved with these kids, and why hadn't she told him or anyone else in the family?

After a couple hours of outside play, the kids led their horses back into the stalls and removed their bridles, as patiently and gently as they had put them on. They took turns with a couple of brushes, currying the horses to remove any sweat, and then Genevieve produced a bag of miniature carrots, handing one to each of the kids to feed their horses.

They took turns washing their hands in the barn's sink. Darcy realized they all knew what to do and where to go, as if they had repeated this day many times. When they were finished washing their hands, they turned toward the house and began walking, single file.

"Lunchtime, Doc," Genevieve said, turning to Darcy with a friendly smile. "Are you coming?"

He trotted along behind her, easily catching up. "So this is what you do for a living," he said. "This is your connection to my aunt."

She gave him a mischievous grin. "Are you disappointed?"

"Why would I be disappointed?" he asked.

"Because now that you realize I'm not trying to steal your inheritance, you have to revise your opinion of me. That's an arduous process for a mind like yours."

He smiled mildly, ignoring her barb. "You could have told me, you know."

"Where's the fun in that?" she asked. "Think of all the entertainment you've had trying to figure me out." She gave him another cheeky grin before speeding up to overtake the children, leading the way inside.

Now Darcy saw what all the food had been for. His aunt had set it out on the kitchen table, along with utensils, and the kids began helping themselves, assembling their own sandwiches. He could have made the food while they were working with the horses, but he realized they were having a lot of fun. Probably to kids who survived on hospital food, getting to make their own lunch was something of an adventure.

His aunt Jo was like a different person as she talked and laughed with the kids, circulating among them to ask them about their mornings. Darcy had never thought of her as a maternal person before, but apparently that was because he had never seen her with a group of sick kids who needed all the love and encouragement they could get. With them she was as soft and loving as his own mother, doling out hugs the way she doled out the cookies she was also passing around.

Darcy sat back, feeling touched, humbled, and inadequate. His family was notoriously generous when it came to charity. But when was the last time he had actually given of his time? When was the last time he had taken a hands-on approach with someone in need? Never, that's when, and the thought left him feeling shamed. Aunt Jo and Genevieve had found a way to give with what they already had—horses, time, and a little bit of food—and look how much joy it brought these kids.

He felt Genevieve's eyes on him as she quietly searched his face, probably trying to figure out what his reaction was. Did she think him so hard-hearted that he would somehow disapprove? If so, she was in for a rude awakening. He slipped outside, pulled out his phone, and called his brothers.

CHAPTER 6

The next morning Darcy was livid when he saw Genevieve arrive on her bicycle.

"I thought I told you not to ride your bike here anymore," he said, striding out of the barn to glare at her, hands on hips.

She hopped off her bike with a laugh. "That's the beauty of our relationship, Doc. You can tell me all the things you want; doesn't mean I have to listen." She turned toward the house, but he reached out to detain her by grasping her wrist.

She swung on him and ripped her hand from his grasp, her face instantly furious. "I thought I told you to stop touching me without permission."

He frowned as he dropped her wrist. Why was she so averse to his touch? "Did something happen to you?" he asked, his eyes narrowing as he swept his assessing gaze over her. Had she been abused?

"Of course not," she said, rubbing her wrist. "But you're tall and I'm short, and you're a stranger. I don't like being manhandled by strangers."

"Manhandled," he said, aghast. "I barely touched you."

"I bruise easily," she said, still rubbing her wrist with a frown.

He frowned, too. "Let me see," he commanded, taking a step toward her.

She backed up a step and hugged her wrist closer to her body.

He sighed in frustration. Did she really think he would hurt her? Then he compared their sizes, recalled how irritable he had been with her, and realized with chagrin that there was a possibility she might. "Listen," he said, as gently as possible. "I would never hurt you or any other woman. I know I'm a big, clumsy oaf and I try to be cognizant of my size, especially with someone as tiny as you. I was grasping your wrist to hold you back because I wanted to tell you something, but if you'd prefer that I not touch you, I'll try hard to remember. My family is touchy-feely, so it comes naturally to me."

She smiled in the amused way he had come to know. "Your family is touch-feely," she repeated.

"What can I say? The Honeywells are huggers. Now may I please look at your wrist? I am a doctor, you know."

"I think I've heard you mention that before," she said, slowly extending her wrist toward him. There were three purple bruise marks were his fingers had laid.

"Genevieve," he said, concerned. "I didn't even squeeze. I don't think it's normal to bruise this way. Maybe you should go to the doctor."

"I thought you were a doctor," she said wryly.

"You know what I mean," he said, his concern making him sound stern. "Do you have insurance? I could pay for a visit since I'm technically responsible."

"That's very sweet, and also very unnecessary, but thank you," she said. "Now what was it you wanted to tell me?"

"Hmm?" he said, still staring at her wrist with a frown.

"Darcy," she prompted.

He startled and looked at her, trying to remember if she had ever said his name before. Why did it make him feel odd to hear it now?

She waved her hand in front of his face. "Are you in there?" she asked.

He shook his head, attempting to clear it. "What I wanted to tell you was…" The sound of an approaching truck cut off his words. "Never mind. They're here."

He watched as his brothers rolled up in a truck and trailer. When they descended the truck, Genevieve took a step closer to him before shielding her hand over her eyes and squinting in their direction.

"Good gravy, there are more of you," she muttered.

He laughed, resisting the urge to lay a companionable arm on her shoulders. He didn't realize how naturally the desire to touch came to him until he had to stifle it. "C'mon," he said, leading the way toward his brothers.

If Darcy thought the sight of so many Honeywells would work to make Genevieve shy, he was wrong.

"Your aunt told me y'all have some quality breeding programs in Lexington, but I thought she was referring to the horses," she announced. The brothers stopped what they were doing and looked at her in surprise.

"This is Genevieve," Darcy explained.

"Her?" Corliss asked. "She's a little bit of a thing. And you say she's a doctor?"

"She has good hearing, too," Genevieve said. She turned her focus on Brent. At 6'5", he was the shortest brother. "Every litter has a runt, I see," she said. "I wish I could sympathize with you, but in my family I'm known as the tall one. What are y'all doing?" She swept her hand toward the trailer.

"You didn't tell her?" Brent asked Darcy.

"I didn't get the chance. She doesn't often let others talk."

"I'm beginning to see that," Brent said, smiling at Genevieve, but she was already on the move again, going to stand at the end of the horse trailer to try and peer in.

"Did you bring another mini?" she asked.

"No, not a mini," Darcy said. He swept her aside, forgetting he wasn't supposed to touch her until he had already moved her out of the way, and opened the trailer. One of their oldest and gentlest family horses poked her head out, saw Darcy, and walked out of the trailer.

"I happened to hear a couple of the kids say they wished they could ride the horses, but they were too small. Sally's perfect for the job. She's good with kids, and she's very social. I think she'll enjoy the minis, too."

Genevieve's face lit with delight. Darcy stared at the sight, something warming inside him as her blue eyes sparkled, her cheek dimpled, and her hands clasped furtively in front of her. "Now that's stupendous thinking, Doc," she said, beaming up at him. How was it that someone who wasn't exactly pretty could still be so beautiful? It wasn't merely that Genevieve was upbeat. Darcy had been around people who were peppy and they generally annoyed him. No, there was something different about her, something deeper than her easy smile. *Joy.* That was it, the elusive description he had been trying to find. Genevieve was filled with joy so deep it radiated from her, infecting others and spreading to everyone around her like the rays of the sun.

And, like the sun, people were drawn to her warmth. Even his brothers were now gathered around her, watching her reactions as they began unloading the truck.

"But what's all this?" she asked. "Are you building another enclosure for the big horse?"

"Nope," Darcy said. "Wait and see."

"Patience isn't exactly my strong suit, Doc," Genevieve said. Indeed, she was fidgeting from foot to foot, standing on her toes, and trying to see into the bed of the truck.

"I never would have guessed," Darcy said dryly.

"At least let me help with whatever this is," she said, rolling up her sleeves.

"I don't think that's such a good idea," he said, horrified at the idea of her working with him and his brothers. Tiny as she was, they could step on her and not even know it.

She smiled up at him. "It's funny how you thought I was asking permission," she said. Then she bounded into the bed of the truck and began tossing supplies to Everett who gave her an appreciative smile because he no longer had to bend over and reach into the truck bed.

"I don't think this is a good idea," Darcy announced, but no one was listening. His brothers were talking with Genevieve, and whatever she was saying was making them laugh. With a resigned sigh, he went forward, rolled up his own sleeves, and started to work.

An hour later, all the supplies were laid out, and they were ready to begin.

"Are you going to tell me what this is now?" Genevieve asked, addressing Darcy. In answer, he plucked the plans from Grant's fingers, and handed them to her. The brothers stood frozen in anticipation as she unfurled the plans, and they weren't disappointed by her reaction.

"Oh, my," she said. "This is so...they're going to love it! Who drew up the plans?"

"I did," Grant said.

"Grant's an engineer," Darcy said.

"I helped," Everett said, surprising everyone. Everett wasn't one for extraneous conversation, especially not about himself.

"Everett's an architect," Darcy added, frowning at his brother. Surely he wasn't somehow interested in Genevieve, was he? At 6'11", he was even taller than Darcy.

"I think you're all brilliant," Genevieve declared.

Darcy watched his brothers in amazement as every one of them blushed faintly under her praise. "We'd best get started," he announced, jolting them into action. To his chagrin, Genevieve's desire to help didn't stop with unloading the truck. And of course she wasn't satisfied to simply stand on the sidelines and hand them tools. No, she wanted to be on top of the playground, crawling around like a monkey and using the compressor gun to nail things.

"Where did you learn about construction?" he asked at one point, standing beneath her when she was perched precariously on the top of a high beam.

"Africa," she said.

At this point nothing should surprise him, but it still did. "Africa?" he repeated.

"Mission trips," she said absently as she kicked a joint to test it, causing Darcy's heart to trip with fear when she teetered before finding her balance again. "We built things. I wanted to be knowledge-able before I went, so I spent some time with construction crews to learn my way around."

"You spent time with construction crews," he repeated incredulously.

"In Brooklyn. They were very nice."

"You spent time with a construction crew in Brooklyn," he said, incredulous.

"Are you okay?" she asked, pausing in her duties to give him a scrutinizing look.

He ignored the question, focusing instead on her location in case she fell and he had to catch her. "What were you doing in Brooklyn?"

"College," she said, prying up a loose nail before removing a new one from her pocket and pounding it back in.

"You went to college in Brooklyn?" he asked.

"Maybe we could talk about this later," she suggested. "You're sort of distracting me, and I'm on a high beam here."

Darcy squeezed his eyes tightly shut, mentally counting to ten. He had never met anyone who could so quickly cause such a wide range of emotions in him. In the span of a few seconds, he had gone from fascination to admiration to horror to wanting to throttle her.

Not only was she maddening, but her energy was boundless. After a few hours of heavy construction work, she herded the brothers into the house and cooked them lunch. Jo was in high spirits. Though not as soft and motherly as she had been with the kids, Darcy thought she still enjoyed having her nephews visit. He felt guilty that they had gone so long without seeing her and vowed to visit her monthly once he returned home. If they took turns visiting her individually, someone could be there every week.

After lunch, Genevieve was ready to go again. Somehow it was as if she had become their team leader and, to Darcy's chagrin, his brothers looked to her when they had questions about design. What was it about this woman that made even the strongest men defer to her? Once again, Darcy's suspicions were aroused.

Clearly, her interest wasn't money. Darcy was beginning to understand that she rode her bike because she didn't have a car. The van she drove with the kids had belonged to the hospital. Her bike wasn't even new or nice, and he knew she didn't own a phone. Poverty in this part of Kentucky wasn't unusual, but it was generally confined to the infirm or the uneducated. She had a doctorate, and yet she lived like a pauper. The clothes she had worn the day before were more fashionable than her non-work clothes, but even they had looked worn and out of date.

What made Genevieve tick? It was a question bound to keep Darcy awake at night because he couldn't find the answer and it was making him crazy.

Late in the day, the playground was complete. There was a row of swings, a slide, places to climb, and, per Genevieve's request, a zipline. She, Grant, and Everett had spent a long time planning that extra, and now it was finally finished.

"This is spectacular," Genevieve said, bestowing them all with her sparkling delight. Darcy secretly wondered if the kids' reactions would be as rewarding as hers. "Let's go inside and I'll make y'all some supper," she added.

"Oh, no," Corliss replied. "It's your time to rest. I'll cook."

"Maybe I could help," she suggested. "I don't do well with downtime."

"We'll see," Corliss replied.

When they went inside, Aunt Jo couldn't seem to get over her surprise that Corliss could cook. "One of you heathens actually knows your way around the kitchen," she repeated more than once.

"Someone has to keep my wife fed, Aunt Jo," Corliss replied. "She's eating for two, you know."

"A baby," Genevieve gasped. "I love babies. Does anyone else have kids?" She looked around at the brothers.

"Corliss is the only one who's married," Darcy replied. "Brent's engaged and getting married in three months, right around the time the baby is due."

"I guess that means you're next," Genevieve said, turning her attention to Brent.

"Oh, no," he replied. "Haley is too young to have children. She's going to finish college first."

Around the room, the other brothers snickered. Darcy leaned over and whispered in Genevieve's ear. "We have bets going about how soon after the wedding they'll have a baby. So far the farthest taker is ten months."

"Why's that?" Genevieve whispered.

"Because Haley wants a baby and Brent can't seem to say no to her."

The edge of disdain in his tone was telling. She gave him the amused smile, the one that let him know she was secretly laughing at him. "But you would say no if it were your wife."

"Someone has to be reasonable; that's hardly ever the woman."

Genevieve chortled a laugh behind her hand. "Mr. Romance," she whispered.

Darcy frowned. "I am romantic."

"Within reason," she added helpfully.

"What's wrong with being reasonable?" His usual underlying irritation with her was starting to grow. The woman was like a burr under his saddle.

"Romance and reason can't ever go together. They're incompatible. It's not reasonable to send someone a thousand roses, but it's romantic."

"A thousand roses," he echoed. "Who does that?"

"My ex boyfriend. Now *he* was romantic."

"Then why is he your ex?" Darcy asked, peeved.

"Because he wasn't reasonable," Genevieve answered. Laughing at his perplexed expression, she skittered away to help Corliss.

After supper everyone sensed Jo was getting tired. She said her goodbyes to her nephews, and Genevieve walked them outside.

"I can't thank you guys enough for this," she said. "The kids are going to be so happy."

"She thinks it's over," Grant said to Darcy. "What have you been doing to give her the impression that the Honeywells would leave a job half done?"

"What else could there possibly be?" Genevieve asked, practically dancing with excitement.

"Wait and see," Brent replied. They walked to the front compartment of the horse trailer and began setting out supplies. It took Genevieve a few minutes before she could make sense of the pieces, but at last she got it.

"A trampoline," she said, and by the way she jumped up and down they were certain they had made the right choice.

The assembly was so quick and easy that Brent and Darcy were able to do it while the other brothers and Genevieve stood back to hand them pieces and give their own opinions on what went where. Because there were children involved, they had bought protective netting as well as pads for the outside ring and coils. They also set the toy on a spot where the grass grew lush and soft, perfect for anyone who accidentally bounced off. And, sick and small as the kids were, they didn't foresee them jumping too high or too hard. The Honeywells, on the other hand...

As soon as it was assembled, Grant and Corliss hopped on, Genevieve in their wake.

"Let's bounce her," Grant suggested. He and Corliss timed their jumps together for maximum spring, sending Genevieve so high into the air that she topped out higher than the protective netting. Of course she squealed like a happy kid, asking to go even higher.

Darcy sat on the grass and watched, smiling and feeling vaguely anxious, a feeling that was new to him. But she was tiny and fragile somehow. If she bounced over the side, she could be seriously hurt. Of course if he volunteered this insight, she would either be outraged or laugh at him. He chuckled. She was irksome, and she drove him crazy, but he couldn't find it in himself to dislike her. In fact, he couldn't remember the last time he had found someone more intriguing or compelling, if he ever had. Possibly that was because he didn't think he had ever met anyone quite like her, and if his brothers' reactions to her was any indication, he wasn't alone in thinking she was unique.

Rarely did they let down their guards so easily to a stranger, preferring instead to keep up the Honeywell myth—that they were all a bunch of dumb oafs who only cared about horses and food. Even Everett, the quietest of their family, had been talking and laughing with her all day.

"Who's next?" Corliss asked. "I'm getting too old for this."

"I'm tired, too," Grant agreed. "There's a reason these things are for kids."

"What?" Genevieve said. "I'm not tired at all."

"That's because you haven't been jumping," Darcy said, vaulting onto the trampoline.

"You're actually going to bounce?" Genevieve asked, surprised.

"Why wouldn't I?" he asked.

"Because it's fun."

Around him, his brothers laughed.

"I am nothing if not fun," Darcy declared.

"Prove it," Genevieve said, crossing her hands over her chest and smiling up at him from her reclined position on the trampoline.

"Fine. Roll up into a little ball and wrap your arms around your knees," he said. "If I can make you unroll then you lose."

She did as he directed, tucking into a small ball like a pill bug. And then he bounced her. Since there was only one of him, he didn't fear making her bounce too high. His only concern was stepping on her, but he was careful, even if he jumped violently to shake her hands loose from her legs. She was stubborn, clinging wildly to her legs until she started laughing too hard to hold on any longer.

"All right, you win," she called at last as she let go her legs and flopped onto her back, exhausted. Darcy took one more bounce and flopped down beside her.

"What was that? Did you say I'm fun?"

"I said you win."

"I'm afraid I'm going to need a formal statement. Tell me I'm fun."

"You know, if I have to tell you you're fun, it sort of proves you're not," she said.

"I'm going to need to hear the words," he prompted.

"Okay, you're fun, tons and tons of fun, 'Call-me-Dr.' Dr. Honeywell."

He laughed. "I never told you to call me doctor."

"I believe you did," she said.

"I did not."

"That's how I'm going to remember it."

He propped himself up on his elbows and looked down at her. With the moonlight sparkling off her blue eyes, masking her choppy hair and pale complexion, she was almost pretty. "There is something seriously wrong with you, Genevieve."

"Believe it or not you're not the first one to tell me that," she said. He wanted to ask who had said such a thing to her, and why, but she was already gone, jumping off the edge of the trampoline and bounding into the darkness.

CHAPTER 7

The next morning, Darcy was prepared for the kids when they arrived, or so he thought. Before leaving the previous night with his brothers, who had volunteered to take her home, Genevieve had told him more kids were coming.

"But they aren't exactly like the first batch," she had said.

"What does that mean?" he asked.

"You'll see," she said cryptically. And when she showed up in a borrowed church van, he did. A dozen sullen-looking preteens oozed out of the van, scanning the horizon with none of the eagerness the group of kids from the hospital had shown. Their attitude toward Genevieve was different, too. Gone was the unadulterated adoration. In its place was wary acceptance, as if she were on probation and needed to earn their trust or favor.

By their ill-fitting dirty clothes, ratty appearance, and lean skeletons, Darcy figured these were some of the local impoverished. Perhaps they had already been in trouble with the law, but he had the sense they were teetering on the edge of a precipice and could go either way. "Troubled" was the word most psychologists would use to describe them. Genevieve introduced him and he watched the kids' eyes widen with surprise at his height, breadth, and well-muscled physique before quickly being replaced by their commonly shared "Who cares?" expression.

Genevieve tried, she really did. She poured love and encouragement on them without being cloying, and the kids responded to her as well as they would any woman. But it was clear, at least to Darcy, that what most of them needed in their lives was a strong male role model. He debated with himself about interfering as he watched the kids with the horses. Unlike with the smaller, better trained kids from the hospital, these weren't allowed to bridle the horses. The horses were led into their pasture and mingled with the kids, trying as hard as Genevieve to gain their acceptance and approval. And, like with Genevieve, it appeared to be working, at least somewhat. The horses brought smiles to faces, worming their way through hardened defenses. But the horses could only do so much. After about a half an hour, the kids became restless, their eyes shifting over the horizon with a look Darcy knew well from his own childhood; they were looking for trouble.

Almost as soon as he hatched the thought, two boys started to scuffle. Genevieve ran toward them to break them apart—even though both boys were taller than her—but Darcy reached them first. He grabbed the angriest looking one by the back of the shirt and dragged him away.

"Come with me," he commanded. He led him to a spot a hundred yards away. "Stand there," he commanded. The kid jerked free of his grasp and plucked at his shirt.

"What for? I didn't do nothing. You can't punish me."

"Punish you?" Darcy said. "Who said anything about punishing you? I need an umpire, somebody tough who isn't afraid to make the hard calls." He started to walk away, then paused, turning to look doubtfully at the kid. "Can you do it? You're not going to play favorites with your friends or anything, are you?"

"I don't have no friends," the kid said sullenly, though his eyes lit with secret delight.

"Good umpires never have friends," Darcy replied. "At least not on the field."

He went to retrieve the other kid who had been fighting. "How are your knees?" he asked.

"Good," the kid said warily.

"Then you're going to be our catcher. Go stand in front of that guy and don't fight with him; he's the umpire." He turned back to the rest of the boys who were now scuffing their feet in the dirt, excited and trying not to look it. "First base, second base, third base, outfield, outfield," he said as he pointed to different boys. "Everyone else is up to bat."

"But we don't have gloves," one boy called.

"I do," Darcy replied. "For everyone except outfield." Judging by the size of the kids, he didn't think that would be a problem. They were probably too underfed to be able to slam hard-hitting home runs. He went to the barn and opened the storage shed, hoping and praying his aunt hadn't gotten rid of the old equipment. Thankfully Jo was something of a packrat. Bats, gloves, and balls remained where they had lain undisturbed for twenty years. Darcy pulled them out and dusted them off.

"You forgot to tell me where to go," Genevieve said from the sidelines as the boys assembled themselves into a diamond shape.

"Aw, Genevieve, girls can't play baseball," the catcher called, squatting into position.

"I'll have you know I'm an awesome player," Genevieve called.

"Don't tell me," Darcy said. "Training camp with the Yankees?"

"The Mets," she said. Since he wasn't sure if she was kidding, he let it slide. "All the same, he's right. This is a man's game, at least for today. You can be first base coach."

"Then I'll be the best first base coach the game has ever known, for women everywhere," Genevieve said.

Darcy took his place on the makeshift pitcher's mound and turned to the dugout area, winding his finger around his ear. "Women," he mouthed.

"I saw that," Genevieve called.

He turned toward her with a wink. "Did you see that?" he asked.

"Yes, and the first action was more believable."

He laughed and looked around, making sure everyone was in place, and then he threw out the first ball. The game reminded him of the many he and his brothers had played with Aunt Jo. Despite the fact that they had been exhausted from all the many tasks she found for them, in the evenings she had insisted they play baseball. And, what's more, she was always the pitcher, even though she was well into her sixties by then.

As Darcy played with the boys, all the summers at his aunt's began to make sense. Even as they concentrated on the game, he could feel the kids vibrating with energy, occasionally darting glances at the rest of the farm to see what mischief they could find. Though he hadn't realized it at the time, he was sure he and his brothers had been the same. No wonder Jo had worked them almost to death; it had been her only defense against the mayhem they might have caused.

As the game wore down, it was almost time for lunch. Darcy knew what food was still in the house, and he knew it wasn't enough. Boys were ravenous at the best of times. These boys had played hard and were underfed to begin with. Surreptitiously, he withdrew his phone, called the local pizza place and ordered a dozen pizzas to be delivered.

To their credit, the kids didn't complain when faced with one sandwich each, a handful of chips, and a cookie. But when the pizzas arrived, it was as if Santa had showed up with a loaded sleigh. Once again Darcy felt humbled by how such a small act could make a few kids so happy. By their over-the-top reaction, he wondered if some of them had never had a pizza delivered before. And if their appetites were any indication, he guessed not. All twelve pizzas were devoured as if a swarm of pizza-eating locusts had descended upon the room.

Hovering at the edge of the room, Genevieve was smiling, but the smile didn't quite reach her eyes. Darcy suddenly felt bad, as if he had overstepped his bounds. He was the type of person who swept into a room and took control, but so was she. With the two of them in proximity of each other, there was bound to be conflict. He eased his way over to her, picking his way around boys who were literally licking their plates clean.

"You okay?" he asked casually, keeping his gaze focused on the kids. Still, he could see her in his peripheral vision and knew when she nodded.

"Thanks for doing this," she said, and she sounded sincere. "This day has been something special these guys won't soon forget. If there were more men like you..." She broke off, and he wondered if she was embarrassed.

"Why don't you come back tonight for supper?" he invited. "I'll pick you up."

She gave him a vague smile that was neither acceptance nor denial of the invitation before turning to address the group of boys. "Okay, guys, it's time to head back. What do we say to Mr. and Miss Honeywell?"

"Thank you sir and ma'am," the boys dutifully replied. Darcy smiled, thinking how typical it was of the south that even the roughest kids still knew how to observe proper manners.

"You're welcome," Darcy and Jo replied together.

"I'll see you next week, boys," Jo said cheerfully.

All eyes swiveled to Darcy. "Won't you be here?"

"I'll be here," he promised. "But that will probably be my last day." Unable to bear the disappointed looks on their faces, he continued. "But maybe I can visit sometime, and maybe I'll see about setting up some guy stuff for you."

They perked up. "What kind of stuff?"

"You'll see," Darcy said, making a mental note to survey his brothers and see what their favorite stuff had been when they were thirteen. For him, it had been thirteen-year-old girls, but that wasn't a very practical solution.

The boys followed Genevieve out, chattering happily about the events of their day. Darcy couldn't help but wonder where they were going. Were their homes as shabby as some of their clothes? Did the sadness on their faces reflect the brokenness of their lives, or was it simply the first vestiges of teenage angst? He wasn't sure boys suffered from that as much as girls did. At least he and his brothers hadn't. They'd all had pleasant, sunny childhoods that had spilled over into adolescence. Sometimes they were grumpy, but he didn't remember any of them ever being sad. Then again, he'd had every worldly good and the support of two parents who loved him, not to mention all the friendship and companionship he could ever want with his brothers and Ivy.

Before this visit, Darcy had realized he was blessed, but always in a head knowledge sort of way. Now the knowledge settled deep in his heart, making him realize how very much he had to be thankful for, and how very much he had to give. It was time for him to do some serious thinking and soul searching. The only problem was that he wasn't certain he was going to like what he discovered. Was he as shallow and selfish as he suspected? Compared to Genevieve or even Aunt Jo, the answer was yes.

There was one place he could start to make amends. He had neglected his aunt over the years, using his childhood fear of her as an excuse to keep from checking on her. Now he was ashamed to realize that strangers in her community had been doing the job of her family —checking on her, keeping her company, providing for her needs, and caring about her interests. She started to shuffle off as he cleaned up the kitchen, but he called her back.

"Aunt Jo," he said.

She turned toward him with her usual frown, but as he reviewed their relationship, he wondered if she was expecting him to lecture her over something. He had never approved of the mini horses, and hadn't been shy with his opinion on the matter. Now he realized how arrogant he had been to lecture her about something that was none of his business. Why had he thought she needed his help or advice? Because she was single and elderly?

"How did you get the horses involved in therapy?" he asked.

She blinked at him, her weathered lashes fluttering in surprise, then she shuffled back into the kitchen and sank heavily in a chair. "It was something I had thought about a lot and hoped to do. Minis have a good temperament for that sort of thing, you know, but I didn't rightly know how to begin. Then, as if it were providence, Genevieve contacted me out of the blue three years ago. She had recently received her doctorate and wanted to do something different instead of work in some stuffy hospital."

"How did she find you?" Darcy asked, trying not to sound as suspicious as he felt. Had Genevieve purposely tracked down his aunt? If so, what for?

"She wanted to work somewhere in Appalachia, somewhere where she was really needed and could make a difference, though I think she could make a difference wherever she was. Someone or t'other knew someone who knew someone who gave her my name in connection with the minis. I had started looking into making them service animals for the blind or visitation pets for nursing homes. Something." When she paused and frowned, he wondered what she was thinking, but he didn't have to wait long to find out.

"It's a terrible thing to be old and feel you have no legacy, Darcy," she said seriously. "Without children, what have I contributed to this earth? I suppose I'm getting a bit sentimental in my dotage, but I want to feel I've left my mark. That first time Genevieve and I spoke, we knew right away we had the same goal: we wanted to make a lasting impact. She didn't know anything about horses. Still doesn't know much—don't tell her I said so—but she's learning, and she has a real gentle way about her that the horses respond to. She presented me with a whole bunch of fancy research about kids and horses, but I told her I didn't need to see it because I had seen for myself the magic horses could work with people.

"So far she only has the two groups of kids who come to visit, but she's looking for others." She paused again and surveyed her nephew through a squint. "That was a real fine idea you and your brothers had about the playground equipment. I've been thinking about stuff like that, too, but it's hard to be an old woman now and incapable of doing for myself. As long as I'm alive, I'd like this place to be welcoming, the kind of place kids think of as fun and special."

"What about camp?" Darcy blurted. While she had been talking, his mind had been running rampant with ideas for expansion.

"Camp?" Jo repeated, not understanding the direction of his thinking.

"You could turn the place into a camp for sick or troubled kids. During the summer months, you could have week-long camps that would reach farther than this small town. They could work on a scholarship basis, give kids a way to spend time on the farm and get back to nature."

Jo's face crinkled in delight. "That's a real fine idea." Some of the joy fled from her face. "Only I don't think I'd have enough money to do all that. The horses cost a lot, and I've been buying a lot of food and paying Genevieve a small stipend. She has other supporters," she hastened to add. "But I'm the biggest one. Not that she makes much. I don't know how the girl lives, and she's always bringing me food. I worry that her own cupboards are bare, but that's Genevieve; she'd rather go without herself than see someone else in need."

"Let me talk to Brent and see what we can do, Aunt Jo," Darcy said. "The Honeywell endowment may need to shift its priorities a little now that one of our own Honeywells is running a charity."

"We have an endowment?" she asked.

Darcy laughed, remembering a little of why he had felt the need to lecture her so many times. Jo saw little value in money or things, so she had never taken the time to learn exactly how much the family possessed. He supposed it was a good thing his father was an honest man. Anyone less might have put his aunt out to dry a pauper. Instead, Aunt Jo had always been included in their largess, even though it was her brother, Darcy's grandfather, who made the real money in the family when he took his earnings from the first Triple Crown race his horse won and invested it in an oil field in Texas. Since then, the Honeywells wealth had grown well beyond horses, but they still put off the illusion that horses were their bread and butter.

"Yes, ma'am, we have an endowment," he said gently.

"Well, glory be, if I'd known that I wouldn't have been taking from my own pocket." She narrowed her gaze on him once again. "You listen to me, Darcy, and you listen real good. You do whatever you have to do to put Genevieve on that payroll and give her a good salary, because if anyone deserves it, it's that girl."

"I'll talk to Brent," Darcy hedged, uncomfortable with the topic shift. It was one thing for the family to fund Jo's pet project, but quite another to start paying a girl they didn't know, one whose motives still might be ulterior. The whole situation was too coincidental in Darcy's opinion. He found it fishy that Genevieve happened to contact his aunt out of the blue coincidentally when she was looking to get her horses involved in therapy.

Darcy vowed to get to the bottom of things. Then maybe his disconcerting inability to stop dwelling on Genevieve would go away, once and for all.

CHAPTER 8

*A*s soon as Darcy decided it was time to go to town and pick up Genevieve, she walked through the door.

"Do you still have the church's van?" he asked.

"Of course not," she said.

"But your bike is still in the barn. How did you get here?"

"I walked, of course."

"You walked? Genevieve."

"What?" she asked, jumping slightly at his accusing tone. She hadn't been paying attention and had no idea why he was angry.

"I told you I would pick you up," he said.

"Why do that when walking is so easy? It's only three miles." She turned once again toward the cupboards, ignoring him entirely.

"Three miles uphill on a twisty, turny roadway where every curve is a blind one. Do you have a death wish?" His irritation increased another notch when she remained staring at the cupboards, ignoring him. "What are you staring at?" he asked.

"I'm trying to figure out what to make for supper tonight," she said.

"I was going to pick up something in town when I retrieved you," he said. "And that's still a good plan. Why don't we go into town and grab something to eat?"

"Let me see what Jo thinks about that," Genevieve said, attempting to dart around him. Without thinking, he reached out and gently grasped her biceps, pinning her in place in front of him.

"Genevieve, please," he said.

"Please what?" she asked in a whisper, looking anywhere but at him.

"Please stand still long enough so I can talk to you. It's like trying to have a conversation with a wounded butterfly. I can tell you're upset and avoiding me, and I want to know why. Did I overstep my bounds today?"

She looked up at then with such an earnest look of gratitude that he was taken aback. "No, Darcy, you were perfect today. I'm really and truly grateful for what you did today."

"Then why are you upset?" he asked. She looked almost like she was ready to cry, and his heart was squeezing in response to whatever was causing her pain. Genevieve shouldn't ever be sad; that much he knew.

She looked as if she was having some sort of mental debate, trying to decide if she wanted to tell him or not. At last she took a deep breath and began. "This program has been my baby from the beginning. My concept, my planning, my kids. I thought it was going well, I thought I had it under control. And then today..."

"And then today what?" he prompted when she trailed off.

"I realize how much is lacking. I can't be what those kids need. I can't be a father or an older brother. I have no idea how teenage boys think. I thought the horses were enough. I thought the food was enough. I thought *I* was enough. But no matter how much of myself I've been pouring into them the last couple of years, it hasn't made as much difference as one afternoon with you." Her blue eyes became luminous with tears, but thankfully they didn't spill over. He wouldn't have been able to stand it if she cried.

"Genevieve, that's not true," he said softly. "I'm the seven-foot-tall cool guy who swept in for a pickup game of baseball and bought them some pizza. You're the loving and devoted counselor who has been with them every week. You don't see the difference you're making because you're with them every week, but I saw it today. They trust you; they look up to you; they need you. Maybe you don't think like a teenage boy. So what? You think like a capable and caring woman who is doing something for them no one else is. Please don't sell yourself short."

She sniffled and gave him a tremulous smile. "You think you're cool?" she asked.

"You know it," he said. He released her bicep so he could raise his arm and kiss his own. "Check out these guns."

She laughed. "Are you really seven feet tall?"

"Now that was a slight exaggeration. I'm 6'10". How tall are you?"

"I'm 4'10," she said.

"You really are a hobbit," he said fondly.

"And you really are a troll," she said in the same tone.

"This troll is hungry," he told her. "Let's go grab Aunt Jo and get some grub."

"With an invitation like that, how can a girl refuse?" she asked.

He laughed. "Tell me about this man who sent you a thousand roses. Was it your birthday? Christmas? Columbus Day?"

"Oh, no, it was something much more special than that; he proposed." She grinned at him because she knew she had piqued his interest. "Jo, the doctor says it's time to grab some grub," she called in the direction of the hallway.

"Aren't you going to finish your story?" he asked.

"Another time, maybe," she said. "From the sounds of it, you would do well to take notes. It seems like you're lacking in the romance department."

"I am not," he said defensively.

"What's the most romantic thing you've ever done for a woman?" she asked, hands on her hips.

To his chagrin, he had to think about that. "I bought one of my girlfriends a horse once at auction."

"Was she rich like you?" she asked.

"What difference does that make?" he asked.

"Because if she was rich and became poor--maybe had her beloved horse taken away and you bought it back for her--then that would be romantic. But if she could have easily bought it for herself and you simply lifted the auction paddle first, then that doesn't count. What else have you got?"

"Are you someone's little sister? Because you're starting to remind me a lot of mine," he said, though that wasn't exactly true. Ivy had attempted to tease him, but she had never gotten under his skin the way this woman did. Genevieve laughed as Jo arrived on the scene, and they went to supper.

Over supper at a small café in town—the only one and therefore it was crowded—the conversation turned to Lou, the mare who was about to foal.

"There is one aspect of the delivery I'm concerned about," Darcy admitted. "Right now she's breech. That could change at any time, but if it doesn't, I'm going to have to flip her. Normally that wouldn't be a problem, but she's so small, I'm afraid my hands are too big for the task."

"I can do it," Jo said. "I've done it plenty of times. I could probably do it in my sleep."

Darcy didn't comment on that. His aunt seemed shockingly frail of late, and she still hadn't recovered from whatever bug had gotten her down. She had always been a proud woman, though, and he didn't want to offend her by pointing out she was in no condition to be in a cool damp barn with her hands inside a horse. He was wishing he had kept his mouth shut and figured something else out on his own when Genevieve spoke up.

"I'll do it," she said. "That sounds fascinating. I've never done something like that before, and I would love the experience."

Darcy wondered if she added the last part to keep from offending Jo. She looked as worried about the older woman as he felt. "That sounds great, but the problem is that Lou could go at any time. If it's in the middle of the night, I'm not sure I'll be able to drive over to get you and make it back in time."

"So move in with us," Jo interrupted. "That's what I've been telling her to do all along," she said to Darcy. "But the stubborn girl doesn't want to make it seem like she's taking advantage."

That was a point in her favor as far as Darcy was concerned. He would have had even more reservations about Genevieve if he had found her living with his aunt, even if Jo did need a caretaker. Still, though, the idea had merit and Genevieve seemed to be waiting for him to comment.

"Please do," he said. "It would be more convenient if I knew you were nearby the moment I needed you, at least until the horse delivers."

"What if she doesn't deliver before you're set to go home?" Genevieve asked.

"She will," Darcy said confidently. "But if she doesn't, then I'll stay until the task is done. I never leave a patient in need, even the ones who can't afford to pay."

Genevieve smiled, dimpling. "Okay, I'll stay until the horse foals."

"It's settled then," Jo said happily. "We'll stop at your place on the way home and grab your things."

Genevieve smiled, but it didn't reach her eyes. Darcy wondered why. Was it as Jo said and she didn't want to appear to be taking advantage? Or was she uncomfortable being so close to Darcy? Did he scare her that much?

He tried to picture himself from her point of view—two feet taller, a hundred pounds heavier, and shoulders the width of two of her put together. Yes, he supposed that would be intimidating. But he had tried to be gentle and careful with her; he would simply have to do better.

Genevieve lived down the block from the restaurant in a tiny house that looked like it had one room. Darcy followed her inside while she packed, intending to carry her bags despite her protests, and found there were three rooms and a bathroom, though they were all tiny.

She didn't have many possessions, but what there was reflected her. Many of her decorations looked as if they had personal meaning —conch shells, some pebbles in a glass jar, and a copy of a Brooklyn street sign. There were pictures scattered about. One in particular drew his interest and he plucked it from its perch on the end table for closer inspection. There was a woman who looked like Genevieve, but different. He wondered if it was her sister. They had the same blue eyes, but this woman had long lustrous hair, brown in color but generously kissed by the sun. Her lashes were long and thick, and her figure, though not fat, was lush and curvaceous. He found himself galvanized, staring at the photo and grasping it so tightly it was in danger of snapping. The woman was gorgeous. It wasn't merely that she was pretty, though she was, but there was something about her that was so vital and womanly he couldn't look away.

"Snooping, Doc?" Genevieve asked as she stepped back into the room, but even that did nothing to divert Darcy's attention from the photo.

"Is this your sister?" he asked. *If so, can I meet her?*

"I don't have a sister," she replied. She gently snatched the photo from his fingers and set it on the shelf without looking at it. "I'm an only child."

"Then who..."

"Ready?" she interrupted.

The mystery of the photo would have to wait. He picked up her bags and followed her to his SUV. He had the fleeting thought that maybe the picture was Genevieve, but quickly dismissed it. No one could change that drastically in such a short amount of time. Could she?

On Saturday, Darcy and Genevieve worked in the stable together. She mucked stalls while Darcy fed and watered the horses, checking their hooves to make sure they didn't need trimmed. Since they were all wearing their ridiculous little shoes, it was a long process until Genevieve got involved, untying and retying their shoes so Darcy simply had to inspect the hooves and move on. Darcy would have to talk to Jo about the shoes; they were unnecessary. Minis had good, strong hooves, and these horses never left the pasture. He thought the shoes were Jo's way of being overprotective since minis never wore metal shoes, but Darcy found them to be a nuisance.

It was nice working so fluidly together with Genevieve, like working with one of his brothers. She was a fast and efficient worker, jumping into any task with the mindset of getting it done and done well. Since he was the same way, they were finished with their chores in record time.

"Let's have cinnamon rolls," Genevieve suggested.

"If you're expecting me to object, you're going to be sorely disappointed," Darcy said.

She laughed and led the way into the house where she began making the dough. As it rose, she prepared coffee and poured them each a cup while they sat at the table. Jo was still asleep, and that in itself was cause for concern.

"I'm worried about her," Genevieve said. There was no need to explain who "her" was; they both knew she was referring to Jo.

"How long has she been like this?" Darcy asked.

"Too long. First she had a cold, and then she had a stomach virus. She hasn't been able to bounce back from either one and she's been sleeping more and more. Sometimes when she thinks I'm not looking, I'll catch her rubbing her hand over her heart. I can't get her to go to the doctor." There was genuine fear in her eyes.

"You really love her," Darcy observed.

"She's the only family I have," Genevieve said. "We're two of a kind, and we look out for each other."

"How did you find her?" Darcy asked.

"I was researching different areas in Kentucky when her name popped up on a website."

"Jo's name came up on a website?" Darcy asked incredulously. His aunt didn't even own a computer.

"Her church had an outing here, and there were pictures of the kids with the horses. The pastor posted it on the church's site and wrote a couple paragraphs about Jo, about what a special woman she is. I had a good feeling about her, and when I called and we spoke, well, we both sort of knew it was meant to be."

That was a more reasonable explanation than Jo's—that Genevieve had magically plucked her from the thousands of horse farmers in the state. Pictures would certainly show the farm was an ideal place for doing therapy horse work, as would the pastor's description of Jo.

"Initially were you intending to work with animals?"

"To be honest, I didn't know what I wanted to do. I had the sense that when I found it I would know, which is a scary way to think when you have a whole heap of college loans breathing down your neck. But I wanted to follow my passion, and my passion rarely leads me to an institution. I'm a bit too unconventional for that."

"Do your parents approve of your career choice?" Darcy asked.

"I would like to believe they would. They died my senior year of college when I was eighteen."

The horror of her parents' death was overshadowed by the second half of her statement. "You were a senior in college when you were eighteen?"

"Try fitting in when you're 4'10", fourteen, and a college freshman. Needless to say I followed the old 'physician heal thyself' adage and chose to work with disenfranchised kids. My parents were wonderful when they were alive, though. They provided me with a strong sense of self that helped me survive their passing."

"So, to clarify, you started your doctoral program at eighteen."

"I'm afraid so. I received a fellowship, but it didn't cover all my expenses, hence the loans. I graduated at twenty three, and I've been here ever since."

Darcy had no reply to that statement. She'd lived a full, fascinating life, and she was only twenty six. She rose and began rolling out the dough, slathering it with butter, sugar, and cinnamon.

"And while you were getting your doctorate, you went to culinary school," he said.

"In the evenings. I thought if psychology didn't work out, it would be nice to have something to fall back on. And, really, it was a stress reliever."

"Sure. I don't know why I didn't think of getting an associate's degree while I was in vet school."

She threw him a cheeky grin over her shoulder. "What about you? Is being a vet your every dream come true?"

"I suppose," he said.

"That doesn't sound convincing."

"No, it is. I was born into a horse family. They're in our blood, so I always knew I was destined to work with horses in some way. Veterinary medicine seemed the best route."

"Why?" she asked.

"Why what?"

"Why become a vet? Certainly there are lots of ways to work with horses without becoming a doctor. Jo's an expert, but she's not a vet. What compelled you to take the extra step?"

"I don't think anyone has ever asked me that before. I suppose it comes down to the belief that a mind is a terrible thing to waste. My parents believe strongly that a good education makes an all-around better person."

"A belief we share," Genevieve said as she cut the log of dough into rolls.

Darcy watched as she popped the rolls into the oven and began preparing a glaze. Soon the enticing aroma of cinnamon and sugar wafted through the house, beckoning Jo from her room. Genevieve poured her a cup of coffee, and they all sat at the table waiting for the rolls. Darcy realized he felt perfectly content, and the feeling puzzled him. Rarely had he found such peace away from his family. Granted, Jo was family, but he had never felt peace in her presence before.

The oven dinged, and Darcy's mouth began to water in anticipation of the rolls. It was torture to have to wait while Genevieve glazed them. When he was finally able to eat them, they were predictably delicious and Darcy ate five before his appetite began to dim. That's when he realized Jo and Genevieve were watching him with matching smiles of amusement.

"These are delicious," he said sheepishly. "Sorry, I hope I left enough for you guys."

"No, I'm glad you enjoy them," Genevieve said. "It's nice to be near someone with a hearty appetite. A cook always likes to feel that her food is appreciated."

"Let me assure you it is," Darcy said. "If this whole doctor thing doesn't work out for you, you always have a spot waiting at the Honeywell household. Our housekeeper is getting ready to retire to spend time with her first grandchild—she's Corliss's mother-in-law."

"Your housekeeper is your brother's mother-in-law?" she asked.

"She came to us when Allie, that's her daughter, was a teenager. Allie and Corliss became inseparable and married as soon as Allie graduated college. Then they hit a rough patch and separated for a few years. They got back together six months ago."

"They got back together six months ago and his wife is six months along?" Genevieve asked with another set of raised eyebrows.

"What can I say? We Honeywells are fertile."

Genevieve blushed delicately and glanced down at her rolls while Jo huffed. "Glory be, have some couth, child," she commanded.

"Yes, ma'am," Darcy said meekly, not pointing out that he hadn't been a child for the last fifteen years. "What's on the agenda for today, ladies?" he asked as soon as the air had cleared a bit.

"Nothing is pressing on my plate, but I always seem to find something to do," Genevieve said.

"I'm sure you do," Darcy agreed. She didn't seem to be able to sit still. "If you don't mind, I'd like to teach you to saddle Sally. You're going to be the one in charge of her after I leave."

She bit her lip. "Saddle the big horse? By myself?"

"She's as gentle as any of the minis."

"Okay," she said, but he could see some lingering fear in her eyes. In most other areas of life, she was fearless. He was surprised she should be afraid of a horse, especially one as gentle as Sally, but after they cleaned the kitchen and went to the barn, he began to see why. Unlike with the minis that even Genevieve towered over, she barely reached Sally's shoulder.

"I should tell you I've never been this close to a normal-sized horse before," she said. "I like animals, but I don't have much experience with them. I've never even owned a dog or cat."

"You're going to have to overcome your fear of her," Darcy said. "Sally is a gentle horse, but horses are sensitive to the moods of their masters. If you're reticent, she'll know it and she'll reflect your nerves. Go ahead and pet her."

She reached out a tentative hand and Sally shied away, nickering.

"Don't be shy; you're the one in charge. Here." He placed his hand over hers and led it to Sally, stroking down the animal's long neck in gentle, controlled movements. "Firm yet gentle," Darcy directed. "Horses like to know who's in charge. If a handler lacks confidence, they'll walk all over him. Sometimes literally."

"You're not doing much to allay my fears here," Genevieve said testily.

Darcy chuckled. "I was speaking in generalities. Sally is gentler than most. She's been our family pet for a lot of years, and she's as sweet as they come." When she seemed to get the hang of petting without fear, Darcy began to show her how to saddle and bridle. "I brought a western saddle because it's easier for untrained riders to use. They're larger and heavier than English saddles, though. Can you lift this?" He dropped the saddle into her arms and watched her stagger back a step.

"Sure," she said unconvincingly.

He took the saddle from her and set it aside without comment. "First we're going to brush the horse's back to remove any grit or dirt. Think how uncomfortable it would be for a horse to have a small rock or burr compressed against him all day. After making sure the horse is clean, set the saddle pad on her back like this, starting at the front of her back and sliding it toward her tail to make sure her hair lies down." He demonstrated with the brush and saddle pad.

"Next you fold the stirrups on top of the saddle so they don't hit the horse. Keep the horse's comfort in mind when you do anything with them; they're sensitive creatures. Lift the saddle high and drop it gently. Try not to drop it hard; horses don't like that. Make sure there aren't any bumps in the pad, and make sure their hair is smooth, too. After that you're ready to cinch. Tighten the girth slowly and gently. Some horses bloat for fear the girth will be too tight, but Sally doesn't do that. Don't make it too tight. You should be able to fit a couple of fingers beneath the cinch." He demonstrated by inserting his fingers and giving a tug. "And that's it."

It seemed so simple to him, but when he turned to Genevieve, she looked lost. "I'm not sure I can remember all that," she said.

"That's why we're going to practice. After today, you'll be a pro." He unsaddled Sally and turned to Genevieve. "Do you remember the first step?"

"Brush the horse. That part looked fun and doable."

He handed her the brush and watched as she stood on her toes to try and reach Sally. Right away he could see the height difference was going to be a problem. What came easily to him was a stretch for her. He looked around until he located a chair and carried it over, lifting her onto it.

"Better, but still awkward," he said. "I never realized before what a handicap it is to be so short."

She put her hands on her hips, prepared to give him a lecture, when she realized he was teasing her. "At least I don't have a constant goose egg on my head from running into doorways and light fixtures," she said.

"Lucky you," he said, rubbing his aching head. Twice that morning he had banged his head on a low-hanging doorway.

She smiled and turned her attention to Sally, brushing her back. "I like this part. I could do this all day, I think. It's relaxing."

"Sally likes it, too," he said, pointing to the horse's eyes which were closed in ecstasy.

"You like that, girl?" Genevieve asked. In reply, Sally gave an answering whicker. Darcy felt satisfied that she and the animal were developing a good rapport and that Genevieve had lost her fear, but he still had concerns about the saddling process. It was awkward for her to have to jump from the chair, retrieve the pad, haul it up to the chair, and deposit it on Sally. Her arms were too short to reach Sally's other side, so she had to drag the chair to that side to smooth the pad. Then it was almost painful to watch her try and haul the heavy saddle onto the chair, to say nothing of seeing her try to deposit it on Sally's back. In an effort to place it gently instead of drop it, she seemed to be straining with all her might. For a beginner, she did a good job, but Darcy was still worried. Maybe he wouldn't be able to leave Sally after he went back to Lexington. She was definitely too much horse for Genevieve to handle.

"That didn't go well, did it?" Genevieve asked.

Darcy held out his hand to her, but she ignored it and hopped off the chair on her own.

"You did great," he said. "Especially for a beginner."

"Yes, but you're still worried," she guessed.

"You're very little," he said by way of an explanation.

"I can do it," she insisted stubbornly. "I don't want my size to be a deterrent for the kids. I'll practice until I get it perfectly. I need to develop my muscles a little more."

"Genevieve, don't be so hard on yourself. It's not your fault you're petite. I should have thought of that in the first place and not brought Sally here."

"No," Genevieve said vehemently. "It was a great idea and the kids are going to love her. The minis already love and worship her as some type of giant deity. She fits here, and we're going to keep her. I'll practice the saddling until I can do it perfectly and everything will be fine."

Darcy wanted to roll his eyes. He wasn't sure he had ever encountered her brand of perfectionism before. She seemed to think that if only she worked hard enough at something she could master it, not taking into account that sometimes life had other ideas.

"Darlin', you need to take a cue from a middle child: sometimes life doesn't cooperate the way you want, and that's okay."

"Did you call me 'darlin'?" she asked, her lip curled in distaste.

"This is Kentucky; women and endearments go hand in hand."

"This is the twenty-first century; sexual harassment and lawsuits go hand in hand," she replied.

"What's so bad about using a term of affection for a member of the opposite sex? I don't understand why y'all get so up in arms about it."

She shrugged. "I don't either. I was playing devil's advocate. I think it's sort of cute. Don't tell my sociology professors. They would take away my feminist card."

"Ugh, feminism," he said.

"Hey, feminism may go to the extreme sometimes, but its inception was necessary at a time when beating a woman was seen as proper punishment for a misbehaving wife. If men hadn't become so oppressive, women would never have felt the need to find our own voice. So, really, you could say that men are responsible for the rise of feminism."

Darcy smiled. "You love a good debate, don't you?"

"More than anything in the world," she replied earnestly. "The open exchange of ideas is the foundation of any great society."

"Okay then, here goes," he said, launching into his beliefs about the pros and cons of feminism. And that was how they spent the afternoon, debating. Darcy had to admit he was having fun. Outside of his brothers, he had never been able to have a deep discussion that didn't lead to an argument. In his experience, most people—and women especially—were so vested in their opinions that they could never seem to debate the issues without emotion getting involved. But Genevieve was the exception. She stuck to the issues, never once becoming angry or raising her voice. And, not only that, but she was able to concede the point if she felt he had won an argument.

All in all, it was the most fun he'd ever had arguing with a woman. Genevieve was intelligent, articulate, and objective. He began to understand why ancient cultures had enjoyed a good debate so much. His mind was firing on all cylinders as he tried to keep pace with her, culling from everything he had ever learned to try and win his point. Likewise Genevieve seemed to be having as much fun and, more importantly, she wasn't taking the debate personally. He had the errant thought that she would fit in well with his family and quickly snuffed it, not understanding why such a thought would pop into his head in the first place. His brothers had already proved they liked her. He suspected Everett was half in love with her already.

They argued as he made his rounds with the horses, checking Lou for signs of labor. At last as the sun was beginning to set, they called a truce for the day, heading inside to check on Jo and make supper.

<h1 style="text-align:center">CHAPTER 10</h1>

"Luke called while you were outside," Jo announced as soon as they entered the kitchen.

Genevieve perked up. "Did he say what he wanted?"

"No, but if I had to guess, I would say it's about a certain dance next week," Jo said.

"Jo, are you matchmaking?" Genevieve asked, pretending to be aghast.

"No, but I do think you should go if he asks you, honey. You need to go and have some fun."

Genevieve bit her lip. "I'm not even sure I have a dress that fits anymore." She sighed before quickly forcing her expression into her usual sunny smile. Darcy watched, not understanding the exchange. He felt like there was something he was missing, but he didn't know what, and no one felt inclined to fill him in. One question was easy to answer, though.

"Is that Luke guy your boyfriend?" he asked, remembering the guy from the hardware store and his overly intense interest in Genevieve.

"No," Genevieve said.

"Not for lack of trying on his part," Jo added. "Genevieve plays hard to get."

Genevieve gave her an impish smile, but otherwise made no reply.

Darcy tried to imagine a string of beaux pining for Genevieve. Granted, she had an adorable personality and she was a lot of fun. That alone could be an inducement for wanting to date her. But he didn't kid himself that men weren't visual creatures, and there wasn't a whole lot in Genevieve to recommend. She had pretty eyes, and he liked her dimple. But her body was that of a twelve-year-old boy, her hair was too short and too choppy, and her complexion completely lacked color. Maybe he was shallow. Maybe other men were able to see around her outward appearance to her shining personality, which was possibly the best he had ever found in a woman. Caring, loving, smart, and funny, she was as interesting as she was sweet. If she were a foot taller and a whole lot cuter, she would be his ideal woman.

"There's a dance?" he asked.

"Next Saturday," Jo supplied. "You should go, too. Live and enjoy life while you're young."

Darcy smiled without reply, knowing that a country dance in a strange town was the very last place he wanted to be in a week's time, especially because it would be his last night here before leaving on Sunday.

As soon as supper was over, Jo went to bed. Darcy and Genevieve watched her walk to her room with matching worried frowns. "When was the last time she was at the doctor?" Darcy asked.

"Last month," Genevieve replied. "I made the appointment and forced her to go, but she wouldn't tell me what he said."

They cleaned up the kitchen in silence, their minds still on Jo. "I'm going to check Lou again. Want to tag along?" Darcy asked.

"Sure, I'll tag along," Genevieve replied, her tone teasing.

"Are you making fun of me, Genevieve?"

"Always, doctor," she replied.

"I'm beginning to get that." They were silent while Darcy examined Lou, pressing a stethoscope to her belly to listen. He ran his hands along her flank, pausing to press every once in awhile. "She's not in labor yet, and the foal is still breech. I feel like she could go at any time, though. I'm going to have to start getting up in the night to check on her."

"I could do it if you told me what to look for," Genevieve volunteered. "I don't sleep much anyway."

"Most things are something a trained vet or experienced horse person would know to look for, but you can check her teats to see if they're dripping milk. If so, that usually means she'll foal within a day or two."

Genevieve bent over to look under the horse. "They look full."

"They fill a week or two before delivery, but don't usually start leaking until the end," Darcy explained.

"Poor thing," Genevieve said, straightening. "She looks miserable."

"I'm sure she is," Darcy said. "She's so tiny. There probably isn't anywhere for her foal to go in there." He gently patted the horse's side, catching Genevieve in his peripheral vision. No doubt it would be the same for her when she had children. She was so tiny she would probably begin to show the first week and be miserable for the remainder of her pregnancy. With a frown, he directed his eyes back to the mare. What an odd thought to have about a woman. He chalked it up to his medical training that made him curious about all aspects of an animal's health, human or not. Still, it was disconcerting to think of Genevieve having kids. Not that she wouldn't make a good mom. She would be an excellent mother, caring, fun, and involved.

He shook his head to clear it. What was wrong with him? What had led his thoughts along this path?

"You okay, Doc?" Genevieve asked.

"Fine," Darcy said. Standing, he moved to the sink and washed his hands. "Want to jump on the trampoline?"

"Sure," she replied. It was a perfect summer night—pleasantly cool with a high moon and many stars. Genevieve vaulted onto the trampoline and began to gently bob up and down.

"If you would give me the chance, I would help you up," Darcy said, hopping up to jump lightly beside her.

"Why? I made it okay."

"I don't know, it's the gentlemanly thing to do. My mother was a stickler about instilling proper manners."

"Why do your proper manners have to preclude me from doing things I'm perfectly capable of doing?" she asked.

"I'm too tired to debate with you again," Darcy said. "I need another eight hours of sleep before my brain will be ready."

"Spoilsport. Fine, let's jump then." They tried jumping next to each other, but couldn't get the rhythm right. Since Darcy was bigger, he kept jostling Genevieve into the protective netting until he reached out and took her hands, grasping them lightly in his so they could jump together. They jumped gently, neither one feeling the desire to bounce high. Eventually they began twisting back and forth, turning in a circle around the trampoline.

"This is fun," Genevieve commented breathlessly.

"It's almost like dancing." He paused. "Why don't you want to go to the dance on Saturday? Jo's right—you should go."

"I didn't say I didn't want to go. If Luke asks, I probably will."

"What's between you two?" Darcy asked.

"Friendship," she replied.

"That's it?"

She tried to shrug but couldn't when he was holding her hands. "He'd like it to be more, but I'm not interested in dating anyone right now."

"Why not?" he asked.

"Someone's nosy tonight," she said.

"Not only tonight," he said.

She smiled, but didn't answer the question. "What about you? Is there a special lady in your life, and is she a giant like you?"

"I met someone recently and I suppose to you she might look like a giant. She's 5'10". Her name is Vivian and her family raises horses in Virginia."

"How serious is it with Vivian from Virginia?" she asked.

"Now who's nosy?" he replied, giving her hands a squeeze. "To answer your question, we haven't been out yet, but I have a good feeling. She has a lot of qualities I'm looking for."

"Meaning she's pretty," Genevieve guessed.

"I'm not that shallow," Darcy protested.

"You're a man; they're *always* that shallow."

"Just for that…" he said, trailing off and letting go of her hands. He plopped hard onto the trampoline, sending her flying high in the air.

She laughed gleefully, landing hard and sending him a couple of inches into the air. "Let me bounce you," she insisted.

"Good luck," he said, knowing she wouldn't be able to do it.

"I can do it," she said. She jumped up and down as hard as she could a few times, but Darcy never got more than three inches off the trampoline. She put more into it, trying harder, but she tripped over him and fell, sprawling across his chest.

"It's not normal to be so large," she said, panting.

"It's not normal to be so small," he said, watching with interest as she attempted to raise herself up and roll away from him. For an instant, he was tempted to rest his hand on her back and keep her there, but he resisted the impulse.

I must be really lonely for female companionship, he thought, trying to remember the last date he'd had. "When's the last time you were on a date?" he asked.

Genevieve lay on her back beside him, staring up at the stars. She sighed. "It's been almost a year now. That was when my boyfriend proposed."

"Why did you say no?" he asked.

"I had my reasons. What about you? When was your last date?"

"Four months ago."

"Why didn't it work out?"

"I don't know," he said, perplexed. "I always think things are going to go well, but they never do. To be honest, I'm starting to doubt myself."

She gasped in mock horror. "Not Doctor Honeywell."

"It's true," he said gravely. "I'm thirty, almost thirty one, and I've never been in a serious relationship. For a while it didn't matter because none of us was settled, but now Brent and Corliss have found someone, and the pressure is on."

"Here's a hint: don't tell any of this to Vivian. Women don't like to feel like they've been selected simply because it's time to find someone." She pointed to the sky. "There's Lyra, the harp, and Cygnus, the swan."

"How did you get to be so smart, Genevieve?" Darcy asked.

"I was born that way," she said. "When I was three, I beat my dad at chess and no one had ever taught me to play. My parents had me tested and I was off the charts. At four, I started school, only I began second grade. It was…not fun. You know how kids are. Eventually my parents withdrew me and homeschooled and I graduated when I was fourteen." She gave a mirthless chuckle. "Most of my early childhood memories involve frustration. You have no idea what it's like to have a mind that's so far in advance of your body. I could solve puzzles in my head, but I lacked the dexterity to put them together. I could see words I wanted to write, but I couldn't hold a pencil properly."

"I had the same problem in reverse. People always thought I was older. By the time I was twelve, I was taller than my teacher. But I had my brothers, and they were in the same boat. I guess it's why we're so close. We were freaks together: the too-tall Honeywells, too rich to associate with any kids from town."

"Are you trying to tell me you were a poor little rich boy?" she asked. "Because I have to tell you I'm a bit short on sympathy for you."

He smiled. "Nah, my childhood was awesome. I wouldn't change a thing about it."

"I wouldn't, either. The ostracism made me a stronger person, and it's fun to have been able to study so many different things. I enjoy knowledge. When you're a kid, though, and in the midst of it, the world can seem pretty dark. If I could convey one message to the kids I deal with, it's that the pain they're suffering is temporary."

"Except the kids from the hospital," Darcy said. "Pain might be all they know in life."

"Even that sort of pain is temporary. Eventually they'll be free."

"You mean like heaven?"

"Yes," she said. "Don't you believe?"

"I believe," he said. They were quiet a few minutes, looking at the stars. He nudged her with his elbow. "Tell me more about the constellations, super computer."

She ignored his barb and began pointing to the sky, telling him not only the names of the stars, but also the legends that went with them. Darcy lay silently listening, that odd feeling of contentment creeping over him again, but this time he was too caught up in listening to Genevieve to analyze it.

"Genevieve," Darcy whispered some time later.

"Hmm," she answered, sounding sleepy.

"What happened to your parents?"

"Plane crash," she said. "My father was flying."

"Where were you?" he asked.

"In the back seat," she said softly.

Darcy's mouth opened in astonishment, but no sound came out. She had survived a plane crash? And not any crash, but one that killed her parents.

"I'm sorry," he said at last.

"Thank you," she answered in the same soft tone.

He wished he had more comfort to give. If he knew her better, he would hold her hand, hug her, or put his arm around her. He might have done that anyway, but something held him back, and he wasn't sure what it was. At last he realized it was fear. Genevieve had already rejected his touch twice, telling him in no uncertain terms not to touch her again. Then he hadn't known her; she had been some annoying pint-sized girl, of no importance to him whatsoever. But now he was beginning to know and care about her, and he didn't want her to reject him, so he didn't try to reach for her. They lay in comfortable silence for a long time, until the outside air reached the dew point and the trampoline became wet. Then they jumped down and went quietly inside.

CHAPTER 11

The next morning was church, and Jo insisted on attending. Despite the fact that she seemed weak, neither Darcy nor Genevieve tried to talk her out of it. She hadn't been out of the house in a while, and they thought the outing and social interaction might do her some good.

She sat in the middle between Darcy and Genevieve because Darcy, aware of how small churches operated, had no interest in making Genevieve the center of gossip for sitting next to a strange man. As it was, he was sure speculation would run rampant about them, especially when people learned Genevieve had moved into Jo's house.

After the service, they filed down to the café, along with every other churchgoing person in the community. Darcy had to try not to laugh that they had a long wait for food that could be described as mediocre at best. He stood back and watched as Genevieve circulated among the waiting crowd, stopping to talk to everyone before pointing them toward Jo. Then whomever Genevieve finished with would make his or her way over to Jo for polite conversation. Darcy had never thought of his aunt as a social creature, but she was certainly eating up the attention, introducing him as her veterinarian nephew with something that sounded a whole lot like pride.

Darcy made polite conversation with the natives, trying hard to understand their overly twangy accents. How three hours in the same state could make such a difference he didn't know, but it did. Maybe it was because, as Jo had pointed out earlier, he was now in Appalachia. It was an area that had remained isolated from the rest of the country by its dangerous back roads and steep hills. Either more of the original culture had been preserved, or less of the outside world had been able to make its mark, or a combination of both. Whatever the reason, Darcy always felt a bit like he was in a foreign country whenever he came to visit.

He kept one eye on Genevieve, noting the way people responded to her as if she were their long-lost daughter. And Genevieve responded in kind with a hug and smile for everyone, as if each person she encountered was the center of her universe. She had a way of making people feel good, a rare quality in Darcy's opinion. When he first met her, he thought maybe she was like a salesman who memorized names and pertinent facts as a way of schmoozing customers. Now he realized she genuinely cared about people. He watched as Luke, the guy from the hardware store, approached her, grasping her elbow to lead her to a less crowded corner. Though the action was hardly necessary. Everyone in the restaurant turned to watch them anyway.

Genevieve leaned against the wall, her arms crossed over her chest as she smiled up at Luke. They were turned to the side, so Darcy could see his expression, and he was smiling, too. He braced his palm against the wall so he leaned over her at an angle. He said something and Genevieve responded, laughing. She reached out to lightly tap his stomach and he shook his head, still smiling. It hit Darcy as he watched the little interplay that, not only was Genevieve flirting, but she was good at it. Poor Luke thought he was in control of the conversation, but it was obvious by their expressions and body language that Genevieve had him reeled in and dangling like a fish.

Their table was called and Genevieve parted ways with Luke, leaving him staring after her as she walked away. Darcy politely held chairs for her and Jo, tucking Genevieve in last.

"Are you going to the dance this Saturday, Dr. Porter?"

"A lady never discusses her dates with another gentleman," Genevieve replied, coquettishly hiding her face behind her menu.

Darcy chuckled. "That boy is besotted."

"That 'boy' is your age," Genevieve informed him.

Darcy frowned, though why that information should bother him he didn't know. He had thought Luke was in his early twenties, still a kid. "And he still works at the feed mill?" Darcy asked, lowering his voice to a whisper.

"It's his family's feed mill," she replied, also in a whisper. "That doesn't bother me. What bothers me is that he's thirty and still unmarried. When a man gets to be that age and remains unattached, you begin to think something must be wrong with him. Don't you think?" She looked up at Darcy with mock innocence before covering her mouth with her hand. "Uh-oh. You're thirty and unmarried. I've really stepped in it now."

"You're the most impudent little psychologist I've ever met," Darcy said.

"If you've known a lot of psychologists, that might explain why you're still single. But, take heart, there's no shame in mental illness, Doctor." She patted his hand.

"Someone needs to tan your backside, Genevieve," he whispered while Jo studied her menu and studiously ignored their banter.

"Are you volunteering?" Genevieve whispered, bestowing on him the same flirtatious smile she had used on Luke.

"Can't you at least be good on the Lord's day?" he asked.

"He made me this way," she replied. "I'm simply glorying in His creation."

The waitress arrived then, cutting off any chance for a reply. Darcy studied Genevieve and Jo as they placed their orders. In some ways, they were remarkably alike. Being a Honeywell, Jo was tall. Her features were masculine, and Darcy had never known her to wear a dress. Even though she was old fashioned and even though they had gone to church, she was wearing conservative wool pants and a light sweater in lieu of a dress.

Genevieve, not even registering at five feet, had delicately feminine features, but she was also covered up in pants, a shirt, sweater, and lightweight scarf. She had applied makeup today, adding more color to her otherwise colorless face, but Darcy still frowned.

"You know it's August," he said, leaning over to speak softly in her ear. "Aren't you warm?"

She shook her head. "My inner thermostat is off kilter. I'm always cold."

"I'm always warm. It's a Honeywell thing; we run hot," he commented.

"Lucky you," Genevieve muttered, cupping her hands around her mug of hot tea and hunching forward.

"Here," Darcy said as he removed his suit jacket and draped it around her. The largeness enveloped her, making her look even more like a small child.

She shuddered and smiled, drawing it closer. "Thanks."

Jo asked about Lou, and they spent a while talking horses. Jo hadn't been out to see her horses in a few weeks. The barn was a long walk from the house. Genevieve suggested dropping her at one end of the barn and picking her up at the other with the car so she would only have to walk the length of the barn. Jo's eyes shone with excitement and anticipation, making Darcy feel bad that he hadn't seen how much Jo was missing her animals. If they were therapeutic for sick children, certainly they could be therapeutic for a sick older woman, too. He made a mental note to try and get his aunt to the barn more often.

Darcy insisted on paying for lunch, to Genevieve's chagrin. "Why on earth would you pay for me? I'm not your guest or employee," she said.

"It's the proper thing to do," he said, not wanting to tell her it was because he knew she couldn't afford to eat out very often. Poor and proud could be a lethal combination.

Jo was in high spirits as they drove home. Darcy dropped her and Genevieve at one end of the barn, drove to the other end, and parked before going into the barn to check on Lou.

The horses were as excited as Jo, prancing around their stalls and whickering in delight. Jo paid each of them special attention and fed them a raisin, even Sally who looked as excited as the minis. Genevieve had been right when she said that the minis looked up to Sally as some sort of supreme being. Most of them had apparently never seen a full-sized horse before, and they were in awe of the larger horse. Sally seemed to feel their appreciation, and it had given her a new lease on life. She was more energetic than Darcy had seen her in years.

As she reached the other end of the barn, Jo's energy began to flag. Darcy and Genevieve helped her to the car and then into the house when they reached it. She went straight to her bedroom for a nap while Darcy staked out the couch and turned on a game. Genevieve went to her room and returned a few minutes later with a large book. She curled up on the opposite end of the couch with the book, covering herself with an afghan.

"What are you reading?" Darcy asked during a commercial.

"A book about ancient Greece," she said.

He glanced at the title, doing a double take. "Is it actually written in Greek?"

"Mmm, hmm," she answered absently as if reading a book in Greek was an everyday thing. Maybe for her it was.

"How many languages do you speak?" he asked.

She tipped down the book and glanced at him overtop it. "Fluently?"

"Sure, let's go with fluently," he said.

"Five," she replied, resuming her reading.

"Five," he murmured, shaking his head. "How does such a large brain fit in such a tiny head?"

Genevieve laughed, extending her foot to poke her toe in his ribs without taking her nose out of her book. "How many languages do you speak?"

"Two if you count horse."

Genevieve laughed again. "Talking to the animals will get you in trouble, Dr. Doolittle."

Darcy smiled, returning his attention to the game as soon as the commercial was over. He woke a while later to find Genevieve staring at him, her book lying facedown on her chest.

"You snore," she announced.

"I do not," Darcy argued, feeling vaguely embarrassed by the accusation.

"The rafters beg to differ. They thought there was an earthquake."

"There are no rafters in here," he said.

"I was talking about in the barn; your snoring was that loud."

"Was not," Darcy argued. He grabbed her foot and started to tickle it, sending her into shrieking fits of laughter as she tried to squirm away from him.

"Stop," she begged. "My feet are very ticklish."

"So I see," he said. They struggled and, though he was larger, she was agile, twisting and pivoting out of his grip like a slippery eel. But, time after time, he caught her again, dragging her back for more. They shifted as the battle intensified so that when someone entered the room and cleared his throat, Genevieve was somehow in Darcy's lap, his arms around her as they struggled for supremacy. They both froze and looked up at Luke who stood in the entryway, staring in surprise.

"Luke," Genevieve said.

"I knocked, but no one answered, and then I heard screaming and came to check," Luke explained uncomfortably, his eyes narrowing on Darcy who still had his arms around Genevieve, pinning her to his chest. Darcy loosened his grip and Genevieve easily extricated herself from his grasp.

"Dr. Honeywell was torturing me," she explained, not sounding in the least uncomfortable or embarrassed. "Thanks for the rescue," she added.

"I came to see if you wanted to go out tonight, Gen. But we could reschedule if this is a bad time."

Genevieve laughed. "Why would this be a bad time? Going out sounds great." She beamed at Luke and stood, turning to Darcy on her way out of the room. "See you, Doc. Please tell Jo I'll be back later."

"See you," Darcy said. He watched as they left, still staring at the door until the sound of Luke's roaring truck rolled away.

CHAPTER 12

On Monday, Darcy woke in a bad mood.

"What's wrong with you?" Genevieve asked as they met up in the barn first thing in the morning.

"Nothing," he snapped. "What time did you get home last night?"

She shrugged. "About midnight I guess."

"It was twelve thirty," he said. "I know because I waited up for you."

"I didn't see you," she said.

"I waited in my room."

"Why? Were you expecting me to come in there? How was I to know you were waiting up for me if you weren't in the living room?"

"I wasn't going to wait in the living room like some sort of..." he broke off, not wanting to say "jealous boyfriend." "Father figure," he finished lamely.

"That's good," she said, nodding definitively. "It would have been awkward to make out in front of you."

"What?" he said, stopping short and whirling around so she had to pivot at the last minute to avoid smacking into him. "You made out with him?"

"Why do you care?" she asked.

"I don't, but Jo is conservative about stuff like that."

"Jo doesn't seem to be the one with the problem here," she said. "And Jo likes Luke. I doubt she would disapprove of a simple goodnight kiss."

"So it was a simple goodnight kiss and not a makeout session?"

"Why does it matter to you which one it was or if it was anything at all? In one week, you'll return to your fabulous life in Lexington and forget all about our little corner of the world. Who cares what happens between me and Luke?"

I care, he wanted to say, but there was no rational explanation for why he should care. She was right; he had only known her a week, and he would be leaving in another week. Who cared if she wanted to live it up with the local feed store guy?

"I think you could do better," he said mildly.

"What's wrong with Luke?"

Darcy shrugged. "You're a doctor and a genius, and he's a store clerk."

She fisted her hands on her hips and frowned up at him. "That's a snobby attitude. Who cares what he does for a living?"

"You should. Could you really be married to someone who isn't as smart as you?"

"Einstein is dead so, yes, I'm afraid I'll have to settle."

Darcy couldn't help it, he laughed. She was so angry and so cocky; he found the combination endearing. "Talk about snobby. Someone sure thinks highly of herself. Tell me, have you written any theories on relativity lately?" he teased.

"I haven't had time. I've been waiting around to stick my hands in a mare. Can you go check her please, so I can get on with my day?" She pointed toward Lou's stall, still clearly angry with him.

Smiling, he went to do her bidding. Genevieve was usually so happy. It was amusing to see her in a temper. Darcy had the feeling not many people were able to push her buttons.

"Well?" she snapped as soon as he finished his examination.

"She's not ready yet," Darcy said. "You have plenty of time to run to the feed mill and visit your boyfriend," he couldn't resist adding.

"Do you really want to go there, Darcy?" Genevieve asked, two livid spots of color filling her cheeks.

"Go where?" he asked, fascinated by her angry display.

"To the place where I might start making fun of Vivian-the-beautiful."

His brow lowered. "What's wrong with Vivian? You don't even know her."

"Oh, I know her," she said. "I read between the lines of your description." She turned and would have walked away, but he caught her arm to hold her back, releasing her before she could tear her arm from his grasp.

"What's that supposed to mean?" he asked.

"Forget it," Genevieve said. "It's better if I don't say a word right now."

"No, I want to hear what you have to say, Genevieve." He was getting really peeved now. What bad thing could she possibly have to say about Vivian?

"Fine. You want to know what I think of Vivian? I think she's probably perfect."

"And what's wrong with that?" he asked.

"Everything," she said, enunciating the word as she drew out all the syllables. "Because perfect means boring, and that's your problem. You want perfection, but then when you find it, you're bored silly and can't understand why. Mark my words—you're going to go out with this woman and realize there's nothing behind the vacant expression, nothing more than a pretty face and overdeveloped glands that make her tall enough to be acceptable."

"Then what's your expert advice, Dr. Porter? Should I go for the ugliest person I can find because she's sure to have a stellar personality?"

"No. I think you need to change your definition of what true beauty is," she replied, and then she turned and stalked away.

They avoided each other for the rest of the afternoon. Darcy wasn't sure why he was so miffed with her except maybe because some of her words had struck home. He knew it was shallow to judge a woman solely on her beauty, yet he didn't seem to be able to stop himself. He wished he had the ability some men possessed to overlook a lackluster face and shapeless body and find lifelong love. But he had no idea how that worked. He was attracted to women like Vivian—tall, beautiful, and curvaceous. And why couldn't he have that? Why couldn't he find a woman who was beautiful on the outside as well as the inside? Who said all ugly women had nice personalities and all beautiful women were mean or insipid? Somewhere in the world there had to be a woman who possessed everything he was looking for. Why should he settle for less?

He determined to say as much to Genevieve, she who supposedly was so open minded, but when he went into the house for supper that night, some of his vim deflated. While he had attributed Genevieve's disappearance to pouting, she had apparently been inside all day cooking. And she had unknowingly prepared one of his favorite meals of pot roast, glazed carrots, roasted potatoes, homemade dinner rolls, and apple pie.

"Someone's been busy," he said, testing the waters to gauge her level of anger. But when she turned to smile at him, he could see no traces of lingering irritation.

"Genevieve, about earlier," he began, but she cut him off.

"Forget about it, Doc. Let's agree to disagree and call a truce."

They ate a pleasant meal together and Jo lingered in the kitchen to talk as Darcy and Genevieve cleaned up. Darcy wondered if it was difficult for Jo to have two people living in her house after living alone for so many years, but she seemed to enjoy their company, even if she did spend a lot of time in her room. For Darcy it was a new experience, too, but in reverse. He was used to living with his parents and five brothers where there was never much solitude or privacy. Being constantly with two women was different, but he found he liked it.

Jo retired to the living room to watch her programs, and Darcy and Genevieve looked at each other, not wanting to spend the evening watching game shows and crime dramas.

"Want to jump on the trampoline again?" she asked.

"Sure." He tossed the dish towel onto its holder and followed her outside. They hopped up onto the trampoline, but neither of them jumped. Instead they sat cross-legged across from each other and talked. Darcy didn't think he had talked so much since college when life was all about spilling his soul and getting to know other people.

"When was your first kiss?" he asked a couple of hours into the conversation. They had shifted positions a few times and were once again sitting cross legged.

"When I was twenty three," she said.

"Twenty three?" he repeated.

"It was the first time I was on the same level as my peers in a way. I graduated with my doctorate, and my boyfriend at the time had just graduated with his undergrad." She paused and smiled. "Believe me when I tell you I've made up for lost time. Once I discovered dating, I wasn't content to stop with once."

"Is that why you said no to the boyfriend who proposed?" he asked.

She shook her head with a secretive smile. "It's really bothering you, huh? Would it make it better or worse if I told you he wasn't my first proposal?"

"How many have there been?" he asked.

"Only two."

"Oh, only two," he said, rolling his eyes. "Why did you say no to the first?"

"Because I wasn't ready to settle down," she said.

"Was that the same reason you said no to the second?" he asked. His leg was going numb. He stretched out on his side and she followed suit. They lay facing each other a foot apart, their heads pillowed on their arms.

"Maybe," she replied, but he didn't think it was. "What about you? Have you ever been proposed to?"

"No, and I've never proposed. It's a nerve wracking thing to ask someone to spend her life with you. I can't believe you've crushed the souls of two men."

"The first one is fine. We keep in contact occasionally. He's married, and he told me once that saying no was the right thing to do."

"What about the second guy?"

"We keep in contact, too. He's a good man. Saying no to him was hard."

"But you had your reasons," he said, trying to feel her out.

"I had my reasons," she said, remaining resolute. "When was your first kiss?"

"I was twelve. The girl was sixteen. I was so tall that she thought we were the same age; I did nothing to correct her assumption."

She smiled. "I'm sure you didn't. I bet you were the envy of all your brothers."

"I didn't tell them," he said.

"Why not?"

"Because it was really special and I didn't want it to become something else."

"Now that is romantic," Genevieve said softly.

As they lay quietly side by side exchanging smiles, an odd sort of tension crept between them, confusing Darcy. This was Genevieve; why should he feel any awkwardness with her? It wasn't as if he was attracted to her. They were friends; that was all. Maybe the old adage was true and men and women couldn't be friends without some form of attraction getting in the way, even if it wasn't physical attraction. He was attracted to her as a person, but he didn't find her attractive. Still, that thought didn't stop him from wanting to reach out and clasp her hand. Maybe that was it—maybe he was simply craving affection. If so, the craving would have to wait; he wasn't going down that road with Genevieve. Not now, not ever.

CHAPTER 13

By Tuesday, Darcy and Genevieve had developed a seamless routine of rising at the same time, working in the barn together, preparing breakfast, spending time with Jo, and going back to the barn. Genevieve insisted on practicing saddling Sally. Darcy stood back, watching with disapproval as she did it over and over again until her arms were shaking with exertion and she was sweating.

"Enough," he declared at last, easily plucking her from the chair with one arm. "I think I know now why God made you so small; it's so someone can physically stop you from killing yourself."

"I can keep going," Genevieve insisted, though she lacked the energy to fight Darcy's grip on her waist.

"Sure you can," he said patronizingly. "But maybe you should try actually riding the horse."

She tensed in his embrace. "By myself?"

"I can ride with you if you want."

"Can the horse carry both of us?"

"Horses are strong, and for family purposes we choose horses that are especially large and strong since we're all so tall. Sally's an old girl, but she's used to carrying a lot of weight."

"All right," Genevieve agreed, sagging against him in relief and exhaustion.

"You're going to have to learn how to mount all by yourself," he told her, then stood back and watched as she arduously tried to ascend the tall horse. At last he couldn't take it anymore and lifted her the final few inches into the saddle.

"I could have done it," she said resentfully.

"Sure you could," he replied in the same patronizing tone he had used earlier.

"I don't like to be patronized," she told him.

"I know, but you also won't listen to reason. I figure it's much easier to agree with you than argue."

"That's a good point," she said after a moment of thought. "I've never been on this side of the farm before," Genevieve commented as they rode on the seldom-used back hill of the farm. "Who mows this?"

"A company my dad hired years ago. Jo wasn't happy. She used to mow all this herself, but it was too much."

"How many acres does she own?"

"About fifty," he said.

Genevieve whistled. "And we're only using a couple. That seems like a lot of waste. Think of the potential here."

Darcy had, though he hadn't shared it with her. After inadvertently hurting her feelings when he intercepted and played baseball with the kids on Friday, he didn't want to stick his nose in where it didn't belong and make suggestions. But there was something else holding him back, and he didn't know what. Surely it wasn't lingering mistrust of Genevieve, was it? This week had convinced him of her honesty and genuineness. Still, he had no idea why he felt almost afraid to talk to her about his ideas concerning the farm. Why had he been able to share them with Jo but not Genevieve?

Sally dipped her head and Darcy clucked, jerking on the reigns.

"Isn't she allowed to eat while she's walking?" Genevieve asked.

"No, but even if she were I wouldn't let her eat those. It's foxtail."

"Is that poisonous?"

"No, but it's not good. The seeds are like barbs that get stuck in her mouth and create nasty lacerations."

Genevieve sighed. "There's a lot to know about horses. I've learned so much already, and it's only a drop in the bucket. With Jo out of commission, I need someone who knows what they're doing. But we certainly can't afford to pay anyone to keep the horses." She bit her lip, frowning.

"You can always call me with questions," Darcy volunteered.

"I appreciate that, but I feel like I need someone here who knows what he's doing."

Darcy felt an odd prickling sensation in his chest. "I'm not staying here," he said.

Genevieve laughed. "Obviously," she said. "Why would you?"

He scowled at the top of her head. He hadn't really thought she was hinting for him to stay, but what had caused the odd sensation, as if something was telling him he was supposed to stay? This wasn't where he belonged; this tiny farm didn't need a full-time vet. His parents' vast spread did. His parents were counting on him. Maybe if he talked to Brent, they could arrange for a local horse person to drop in once a week to check on the horses. Surely they could afford someone once a week, couldn't they? Genevieve was right; she wasn't knowledgeable enough about horses to oversee their care on a daily basis without Jo, and Jo was in no shape to be directly involved in the care of her horses anymore.

"We'll work something out," he said with more confidence than he felt.

"Something always works out," Genevieve said cheerfully.

Darcy smiled. "You're such a little optimist, Genevieve."

"I'm a naturally upbeat person, but there are still times when I have to decide whether I want to be joyful or wallow in self pity. I choose joy."

The words resonated with Darcy. *I choose joy.* Nothing in his life had ever gone badly, making it easy for him to be happy. But what if he had lost his parents in a plane crash? What if he had been alone for the last eight years, living among strangers and trying to make his own way in the world? Would he still be happy? He hoped so, but he couldn't say for sure. One thing he knew for certain was that a lot of people wouldn't. Most people would have thrown in the towel and chosen to wallow in self pity, as Genevieve had said. The fact that she hadn't made him like her even more.

He realized then that she was leaning on him. Somehow in the space of the last few days, she had gone from recoiling at his touch to resting her full weight on him without thought. Darcy smiled, resting his hand on her waist and giving it a light squeeze. She was so small that one hand almost spanned half of her circumference, and he could feel her ribs under his fingers. He frowned, not liking how skinny she felt. There was a difference between petite and malnourished, and Genevieve was too far on the unhealthy side of that scale.

"Genevieve, you need to eat more," he announced.

"That must be something every girl longs to hear."

"I didn't mean it as an insult," Darcy said. "I'm worried about you."

"I'm fine," she said flippantly.

"Of course you are," he said, sighing in defeat. She was so proud and stubborn, she would never admit it even if she was dying. Exactly like Aunt Jo. He cast his eyes heavenward and shook his head. How did he get stuck with two such headstrong females?

On Wednesday, Darcy took Genevieve to the children's hospital. It wasn't an actual hospital—the area was too small and too poor for that—rather, it was a satellite branch of the hospital in Lexington. Darcy felt better knowing the kids were able to live at home with their families; previously he had pictured them living in an institution. They were still poor, though, and the trip to the farm was the highlight of their week.

He left his SUV in the satellite complex's parking lot while he helped Genevieve load the kids in the hospital's passenger van. When he learned that she had sweet talked the hospital administrators into purchasing the van for such an occasion, he smiled. Eventually, she would probably succeed in turning her therapy program into a larger organization, even without the backing of the Honeywell endowment.

She was driven and focused, but also so sweet and genuine that people wanted to trust her with their money.

Darcy wanted to drive, but Genevieve told him he wasn't allowed for insurance purposes. He didn't know if that was true or not, but he gritted his teeth and climbed into the passenger side after offering to find a phone book for Genevieve to sit on.

"I can see over the steering wheel perfectly," she told him peevishly. "I'm a good driver."

And she was. It took him a while to relax, but she was careful and attentive, not even allowing the kids' laughter and questions to distract her.

The kids hadn't seen the new additions to the farm, so when they arrived, they were more excited over the trampoline and playground equipment than they were the horses. For a while, Darcy manned the trampoline—lifting kids up and down—while Genevieve stood at the playground and pushed kids on the swings.

The horses, feeling very neglected, began making their presence known by impatiently stamping their feet and snorting until at last the kids grew tired of the new toys and made their way into the barn. Then they saw Sally and the excitement started all over again. Darcy saddled her and gave the kids rides, two at a time, leading Sally around by her bridle.

At lunchtime, they were exhausted yet ecstatic as they excitedly filled Jo in on all their adventures from that morning. Darcy watched Jo's face fill with delight, and he smiled, glad the kids were bringing her so much joy in her declining years. He tried to picture her life without Genevieve and the children, and it was a sad presentation of a lonely old woman. He would be eternally grateful to Genevieve for giving this gift to his aunt, and he vowed to follow through on Jo's request by taking care of Genevieve after Jo's passing, even if that meant assisting her in finding another placement.

On Thursday Corliss and Brent arrived with more equipment. By now Darcy and Genevieve were practically attached at the hip without even realizing it. But Brent and Corliss noticed, shooting Darcy questioning looks, which he didn't return.

With Genevieve's help, the brothers quickly unloaded the truck and began to assemble a batting cage, complete with Astroturf and pitching machine. Because of safety concerns, it was a softball machine, and they also brought helmets along with new bats and balls. In addition to that, they set up a basketball hoop outside the barn and a volleyball net in one of the unused pastures.

"Someday we'll have to dig it out and fill it with sand," Corliss said as they stood back to admire their handiwork.

He and Brent didn't linger, leaving almost as soon as they finished their work and spoke to their aunt.

"They're so different now that they're attached," Darcy commented, not realizing he was staring wistfully at his brothers as they drove away.

"Falling in love has a way of doing that to you," Genevieve said.

Darcy turned to look at her. "You speaking from personal experience?"

She smiled. "Of course. Hasn't everyone been in love sometime?"

"I don't know," he said, thinking. Had he ever been in love? If he had, it hadn't been the sort of love his brothers had found, the kind that could compel him to change his life or rush home to a woman because he hadn't seen her in a few hours. He felt almost frustrated with them for making him realize what he was missing. Or maybe he was jealous. Maybe both. All he knew was that people around him were changing and he didn't want to be one of them.

CHAPTER 14

On Friday, the local boys arrived again, looking perkier than they had the week before. They spent some time with the horses, took turns with the trampoline and batting cage, and then turned expectantly to Darcy.

"Aren't we going to play ball?" one of the boys asked.

"Sure, but this time Genevieve gets to play," Darcy replied.

"Yes," Genevieve said, pumping her fist in the air.

Not surprisingly to Darcy, she turned out to be a good, if somewhat aggressive player. She stole bases too many times to count, handing her team the win by three points. The boys recounted the game for Jo, embellishing Genevieve's behavior, when Darcy surprised them by saying how often Jo used to play baseball with him and his brothers.

Darcy drove the borrowed church van this time, with Genevieve sitting shotgun as they took the kids home. In some ways, he wished he hadn't insisted on accompanying her because seeing where they lived was proving to be depressing. Some of the houses were so ramshackle that they were merely plywood and tar paper. Darcy wasn't sure how they were even livable, but since about half the homes were in the same condition, he figured it must not be uncommon for this area. The shacks were even smaller than Genevieve's small abode, which was saying something.

"How do they live?" Darcy asked after they said goodbye to the last boy.

"Not well," Genevieve said. "And it isn't merely the poverty. Their family situations are unhealthy. None of their parents seem to understand the value of education or proper nutrition, to say nothing of the lack of affection in the kids' lives. Someday I would love to have some sort of program for parents, something that teaches them a better way."

So much needed done here, and it was one small segment of the country. "How do you keep from becoming overwhelmed by it all?" Darcy asked.

"I try to keep my focus local. If we can make a lasting impact on one kid, then that kid will impact others, and so on. Maybe we're not changing the world, but we can try to change our little piece of it."

"I suppose," Darcy agreed, though he still felt vaguely depressed. "Do you mind if we pick up a couple of pizzas for supper? If I go too long without eating pizza, I get cranky."

"Had you gone a long time without it when you first arrived here?" Genevieve asked.

Darcy reached over and squeezed her knee. "I was not that cranky."

"Serial killers smile more than you did," she said, earning another squeezed knee. As she jumped and tried to pry his fingers off her, he realized how much he was going to miss her. Impossibly in two weeks, she had somehow become vitally important to him, and he would feel a little lost without her friendship. He comforted himself with the thought that he had promised to check on Aunt Jo every few weeks. Genevieve would no doubt be nearby, and he could spend time with her, too.

He wondered if she was having similar thoughts because she seemed quiet and subdued as they ate supper with Jo. She followed him to the barn to check on Lou, and then they transitioned to the trampoline where they once again didn't put up the pretense of actually wanting to jump. Instead, they lay on their backs, looking at the stars. Darcy had remembered to grab the afghan for her because, even though it was a warm night, she was still shivering.

After spending practically the entire week together, they shouldn't have had anything left to talk about, but somehow they did. Darcy had gone to church camp once, and his relationship with Genevieve reminded him of the camp romance he'd experienced that week. It was special and intense somehow, though not technically a romance. They talked for a few hours and said goodnight. Darcy felt as though he had barely closed his eyes when Genevieve called his name.

"Darcy," she whispered.

His eyes popped open and he saw her standing over him in a sweatshirt and pair of shorts, her hair standing up in short spikes all around her face.

"What's wrong?" he asked.

"I couldn't sleep so I checked on Lou. She's leaking milk."

"Oh." He sprang up, intending to bolt out of bed before quickly remembering he was only wearing a pair of boxers. Genevieve must have been thinking the same thing because she backed toward the door, laughing.

"I'll meet you at the barn," she said. Covering her eyes with her hands, she made a show of peeking through her fingers at him.

Darcy laughed, coming more awake now. "Get out of here, peeper, so I can get dressed."

"Normal people sleep in pajamas," she told him before she turned and darted out the door.

He shook his head, smiling, as he felt about for his clothes, throwing on whatever was closest in the dim light spilling from the hallway.

Genevieve stood anxiously at the end of Lou's stall. She moved aside and made room for Darcy as he advanced, brushing by her to enter the stall. Lou shied away from him and whinnied.

"Easy girl," Darcy said gently, running his hand along her flank. He checked her progress and found she was indeed in labor, and the foal was still breech.

"You're going to have to turn her for me," he said, glancing at Genevieve. "Are you still up for it?"

She nodded, looking enthusiastic. He chuckled. "Of course you are," he muttered. He brought over a table and draped it with a sterile cloth, setting out instruments and an extra light.

"What's all that for?" Genevieve asked, sounding worried now.

"If for some reason you're not able to turn her, or if something else happens, I'm going to have to do an emergency c-section. That's a worst case scenario, though. We're going to do all we can to get her through this naturally."

"Okay," Genevieve said, swallowing nervously. "I'll go wash up." She turned to the sink and began washing, jumping in surprise when Darcy came up behind and handed her a bottle of disinfecting soap.

"Use this and scrub like the surgeons you've seen on television, and then we're going to disinfect you again," he said. Then he stood beside her and scrubbed himself all the way up to his elbows, nodding approvingly when she did the same.

When they were well scrubbed, they returned to Lou. Darcy slathered Genevieve's arms with foul-smelling surgical disinfectant. As he was doing so, Lou's water broke.

"She's going to go into hard labor now," Darcy said sounding more urgent. "Now's the time to do this." He slathered the horse with more of the disinfectant and then positioned himself hunching over the animal, motioning Genevieve to stand in front of him.

"You're going to take this sterile string and you're going to tie it around the foal's pastern. That's the long bone above its hoof, sort of like a human shin. Tie it tightly because I'm going to be pulling on it. Do you know a good knot?" He felt a second of panic, thinking he should have taught her a proper knot, but she nodded.

"I know a good knot," she said. Taking a deep breath, she took the proffered string and inserted her hands inside the horse, grimacing at the sensation. "I'm sorry about this," she added to Lou. "It's for your own good. I promise."

"Talking to the animals will get you in trouble, Dr. Doolittle,"

Darcy said softly beside her ear. She smiled and relaxed slightly, sticking out her tongue and biting it as she tied the knot.

"Okay, the knot is tied, and I'm pretty sure it's in the right place. I followed the hoof up a few inches."

"Good. Now I want you to locate the horse's head. You're going to push it back while I pull on the leg, and we're going to flip it. You'll feel it when it's time to stop; it will slip into alignment and you can pull your arms out. Ready?"

"Ready," Genevieve said, and Darcy was heartened by her steady tone. She might be a little grossed out by the process, but she wasn't squeamish. She pushed as Darcy pulled and Lou contracted, impeding their progress so that it took a long time. At last the foal gave a monumental flip, and it was done.

"There," Darcy announced, though Genevieve had felt for herself that the horse was in the right position. She withdrew her arms and went to the sink to wash up while Darcy examined his patient.

"Genevieve, hurry back—you're about to miss it," he called a few seconds later.

Genevieve dashed back to the stall, stopping short when she saw two hooves protruding from Lou. "Is that how it's supposed to be?" she whispered.

"That's perfect," Darcy said, "though I wish she was lying down. I'm going to have to catch it."

The head emerged and Genevieve caught Darcy's arm, her nails unknowingly digging into his flesh as her anxiety grew. The shoulders emerged with more difficulty. Lou looked as if she took a breather for a few seconds before pushing out the rest of the little foal's body. Darcy knelt, catching it like it was a game winning pass, before gently setting it on the soft hay. Lou took a couple of breaths before turning around and lying down next to her baby to clean it. Darcy remained sitting nearby in case either the mare or foal might need him. Genevieve sank down beside him, not realizing she was crying until Darcy pointed it out.

"That was the best thing ever," she said, awed. She bestowed a beaming smile on Darcy, which he returned. He leaned forward—to kiss her cheek? He wasn't sure, but whatever his intent had been, it didn't pan out. Instead he caught her around the waist and kissed her on the mouth, softly at first. Genevieve gasped in surprise, her eyes wide with astonishment. There was a pause when they looked at each other, and then she closed her eyes, practically melting into him as he tightened his grip on her waist and cinched her closer, deepening the kiss.

The kiss seemed to go on forever, until the snuffling noise of the foal once again alerted Darcy to his task. He let Genevieve go, turning away from her. He needed to check his patients again, but it was more than that; regret was already beginning to set in. He moved forward, cutting Genevieve out of his peripheral vision. She remained for another minute, breathing raggedly, and then she was gone, walking away without a word.

<h1 style="text-align:center">CHAPTER 15</h1>

*D*arcy didn't sleep. He told himself he was staying awake for his patient, but that was a lie. Lou and her foal were fine. The truth was that he was too anxious to sleep. What had he done? Why had he kissed Genevieve? Why had it been so amazing? And, more importantly, what was he going to do now?

How could he explain to her that it had been a mistake when he was the one who had kissed her? How could he tell her they had no future together without hurting her? He cared about her, but he couldn't make himself fall in love with someone he wasn't attracted to, and he wasn't attracted to Genevieve, at least not physically.

Maybe, being Genevieve, she would give him a pass and pretend the whole thing hadn't happened. Maybe they could laugh about it to cover any awkwardness that the kiss might have caused. After all, hadn't she repeatedly said she didn't want a relationship right now? He didn't think she was attracted to him. He certainly hadn't received that vibe from her throughout the week, which was probably one reason he had felt so comfortable spending so much time with her. He had the feeling Genevieve wanted to be with him about as much as he wanted to be with her, which was not at all.

The car started—his car—and he poked his head out of the barn to see why. Genevieve was driving Jo to the barn, making Darcy once again feel guilty for not thinking to do so in the first place. Lou was one of Jo's most beloved horses. Of course she would want to see her foal.

Darcy held his breath as they descended the vehicle, but Genevieve didn't look at him. Instead she concentrated on Jo who looked weak despite her excitement.

"She's a beauty," Jo said, smiling at her first sight of the foal.

"What are you going to name her?" Darcy asked, reaching out his hand to offer support when Jo tottered.

"Let's let Genevieve name it," Jo suggested. "She did the hard part with this one."

Genevieve smiled as she looked at the foal. "Is it a girl?" she asked, not looking at Darcy as she spoke.

"She's a girl," Darcy replied. He was trying to read her expression, but she kept her eyes hidden.

"Then I'll call her Alcippe."

"What language is that?" Jo asked.

"It's Greek," Genevieve replied. "It means mighty horse."

"Alcippe," Jo repeated, turning the name over in her mouth. "I like that. It's dignified and fitting for Lou's daughter. She's always been a proud little horse."

They stood for a while admiring the mare until it became clear Jo had reached the limit of her energy. Darcy and Genevieve helped her back to the SUV. Darcy tried to catch Genevieve's eye, but she studiously avoided him.

The avoidance continued through a breakfast of French toast, even though she responded to his questions as he asked them.

"Did you sleep?" he tried.

"Some," she said, shrugging with her back to him as she flipped the toast.

"Genevieve," he started, but the arrival of Jo interrupted whatever he might have said.

Genevieve served them, saving herself for last and picking at her food. Darcy felt like doing the same this morning, and he couldn't remember the last time he hadn't been hungry. Thankfully Jo was in high spirits and carried the conversation through breakfast. She remained in the kitchen during cleanup, denying Darcy the chance to speak to Genevieve, but he vowed to speak to her as soon as he could get her alone.

"I think I'll take a nap," Genevieve announced as soon as she handed Darcy the last dish. She finally looked up at him, but he couldn't read her expression. "You should get some rest, too, Darcy. I know you must be exhausted." For a few beats their eyes caught and held, and then she tore her gaze away, smiling at Jo as she left the room.

Darcy dried the dish and put it away, exhaustion settling over him and making him feel muddled. He hung the towel on the rack and passed by Jo, leaning over her as he went in order to bestow a kiss on the top of her head.

"Congratulations, Jo. She's a fine little foal."

Jo smiled and patted his hand. "Thank you, Darcy, for all your help. I know the mortality rate for minis with that type of presentation."

"I couldn't have flipped her without Genevieve," he said honestly. No doubt his large hands probably would have killed both foal and mare if he'd tried to do the flipping, leaving c-section as his only alternative, and c-sections in the field were definitely a last resort. Too much could go wrong.

"We'd be lost without her," Jo commented sincerely. Darcy squeezed her hand, but he didn't disagree, hoping instead that he hadn't messed things up too badly with his ill-timed kiss.

He slept for what felt like a long time. The house was quiet when he showered and stepped out of his room. He wondered if the women were at the barn, but when he checked Lou and her foal, the barn was empty of humans. As a distraction, he checked the other horses, noting as he did so that Genevieve had already fed them and mucked their stalls. He wondered if she had actually slept or if she had merely escaped to her room as a way to avoid him.

"Do you feel better after you slept?"

Darcy turned. Genevieve stood in the doorway, leaning one shoulder against the frame, her arms crossed over her chest. She was wearing a dress, the first one he had seen on her. He felt a moment of panic thinking she had dressed up to talk to him and then he remembered she was going to the dance with Luke.

The dress, tiny as it was, still hung off her almost emaciated frame. It was white with red poppies and might have been pretty if she had enough of a figure to fill it out. Today she had arranged her hair into wild spikes, a pixie style that suited her small features, and she was wearing makeup. She looked as pretty as he had ever seen her, and he smiled.

"I feel better. What about you? Did you sleep?"

"A bit." She scraped her bottom teeth over her top lip then frowned, apparently remembering she was wearing gloss as she rubbed her lips together. "Darcy, I wanted to tell you…" She broke off, looking toward the far wall and swallowing hard before gaining the courage to start again.

Darcy felt as nervous as she looked. What was she going to say? That the kiss had woken some sort of latent passion in her? Or that she also thought it had been a mistake?

"I wanted to ask you if you've ever heard the story of beauty and the beast."

He blinked at her, wondering if he had heard her wrong. Of all the things he had expected her to say, that hadn't been it. "I'm vaguely familiar. Why do you ask?" he said after some hesitation.

She looked down, nervously twining her fingers together. "In the story, there was a prince. He was cast under a spell and forced to become a beast. Underneath, he was really very attractive, but no one could see it, and then he met Belle. She saw through to the person he truly was, and she loved him, despite his outward appearance. Does this make sense to you at all, what I'm trying to tell you?" She twined her fingers furiously now, probably chafing her skin until it was painful. Her eyes were pleading when she looked at him, and with a sinking heart he began to understand. She was asking him to love her despite her outward appearance, despite the fact that she wasn't physically very attractive. At that moment, he wanted nothing more than to find her beautiful, but he couldn't. She was wonderful and special with a radiant spirit, but he couldn't see beyond her outer shell. He hated himself for it, but he couldn't pretend to feel something he didn't.

Some of what he was thinking must have shown on his face because she straightened in the doorway and forced a smile. "Never mind. Listen to me talking about fairy tales when Luke will be here any minute. I know you're leaving early in the morning, and I wanted to say goodbye. It was a fun week. Take care." Her smile became tremulous as she took a step back out of the barn, and then she turned and fled.

"Genevieve," he said softly, reaching a hand toward her, but it was too late. She was gone.

He finished with the horses, his heart as heavy as his step. When he returned to the house, his guilt increased because, even though Luke was taking her to dinner, Genevieve had prepared supper for Darcy and Jo. It was probably delicious, but to Darcy, who was practically drowning in guilt, it tasted like sawdust.

Jo seemed as serious as Darcy felt. They ate in silence until Jo set aside her fork and looked up.

"I have to tell you something," she said gravely.

Darcy's heart constricted. Was she about to tell him she was dying? It would be nothing less than what he suspected, but he still didn't want to hear it. "What is it, Aunt Jo?" he asked, setting aside his own fork and gripping his napkin in his lap.

"As a rule, I don't meddle. But I need to know that when I'm gone you'll take care of Genevieve, and I know the only way you'll do that is if you know the full story. And you'll see the checks, and you'll wonder what they're for; Lord knows she'll never tell you." She frowned and Darcy's anxiety grew.

"Checks?" he asked. "What checks?" Surely he hadn't been wrong about Genevieve again. Surely she wasn't bilking his aunt for money after all, was she?

"Genevieve has leukemia."

She sat back, letting the words find their mark, and they did, hitting Darcy solidly in the chest and knocking him back. "What?" his voice sounded like a croak.

"She's in remission now, but the chemotherapy was tough on her, not that she would tell you that. She lost all her beautiful long hair, lashes, and brows, along with about twenty pounds she already couldn't afford to lose."

"Is she…is she dying?" He couldn't get a breath. Was he gasping, or was it his imagination?

"I don't know," Jo said, her lips trembling. "It's hard to get a straight answer from her. She would have died if I hadn't stepped in. You see, her insurance was horrible, barely any coverage at all. It paid for a small part of half of her treatment and then stopped. And she let it, didn't tell a soul, didn't say a word. Only when I noticed her hair growing back did I call her on it. I knew she needed six months of treatment, and it had only been three. When I found out she was giving up, I hit the roof and paid for the remainder of her treatments out of my pocket." She finished the last part defiantly as if she expected Darcy to argue with her, but he nodded dumbly, feeling as if he had been hit in the head with an anvil.

Genevieve had leukemia? She'd had chemo, and that was why she looked like she was sick because she actually was sick. How could he have been so stupid? It was right there in front of him all the time, yet he had chosen to ignore it, thinking instead she wasn't attractive. Even on the day he had seen her with the cancer patients and realized how much she looked like them, he had chalked it up to her desire to relate to the kids, not realizing that she actually *could* relate to the kids. The easy bruising, the lack of appetite, weight loss, hair loss, and gray pallor had been blaringly obvious and he, a doctor, had ignored it all.

"She had long hair," he repeated, fastening onto the most trivial of things his aunt had said.

"She was a beautiful girl. Still is, in my opinion, though she's a bit self-conscious of her appearance now. Not that she would say anything or complain, but I know her well enough to know. Looking like she does right now hurts her, but she doesn't put much stock in outward beauty."

Darcy flinched, feeling as if his aunt had slapped him. Of course she couldn't know how much the words hurt. He wished she would slap him or kick him or do anything to punish him for the horrible things he had thought about Genevieve. How could he have been so blind and stupid? Her story about beauty and the beast made actual sense now, and not his own conceited version of the truth. Genevieve had been trying to tell him that she wasn't actually the person he saw. She had been asking him to look inside her and love her for who she was and not how she looked at the moment. She had been testing him, and he had failed. Miserably.

His insides felt like they were on fire. He wanted to go somewhere, anywhere, and escape the horrible pain. What was wrong with him that he had put so much stock in something so stupid? In light of Genevieve's possible death, what did it matter if her hair was short or she was too skinny? What did any of that matter when it came to the possibility of losing her forever?

Too late, the words echoed in his head, making him feel almost sick with panic. *It's too late,* the tormenting words echoed. He shook his head, realizing as he did so that Jo was staring at him in alarm. He wondered if he looked as wild as he felt.

"Where is the dance?" he asked, his voice still sounding like a croaky rasp.

"Downtown at the park." Jo blinked at him a few times. "Will you promise to take care of Genevieve when I'm gone, Darcy? You never said."

He stood, upsetting his chair in the process. He caught and righted it before it could clatter to the floor. "I promise, Jo. I'll take care of her to the very best of my ability."

She nodded, still giving him the wary look, but he didn't stay to try and explain his odd behavior. Instead he dashed to his car and backed down the long lane, forcing his mind to calm before he reached the deathtrap roadway. He breathed slowly in and out of his mouth, feeling nauseated and lightheaded. He had never felt this horrible before, never this guilty or hopeless or afraid. The what-ifs kept running through his mind, and no matter how much he tried to turn them off, he couldn't. What if Genevieve was still sick? What if she died? What if she couldn't forgive him? What if he'd lost her?

He arrived downtown, parking haphazardly across two spaces. Throwing the car into park, he hopped out, not even bothering to remove his keys from the ignition, desperate to reach her, to reach Genevieve.

The music streamed out long before he reached the park. The crowd was large and he caught sight of people swaying. He was too far to see Genevieve, but he resisted the urge to run, forcing himself to walk in measured paces. He reached the edge of the crowd, easily towering over everyone else in attendance as he searched the dance floor for Genevieve. And when he saw her, it was as if his blinders had been removed. He stood still, his mouth opening in surprise. Genevieve was beautiful.

Rationally, his mind told him she looked exactly the same. She was too short, too skinny, and too gray to really be attractive, but none of that mattered. As if by magic, Darcy was able to see beyond all of that to the radiant beauty inside her. She shone with it like a beam of light, her smile lighting her face, her blue eyes twinkling as they looked up at Luke.

Thoughts of the other man drew Darcy from his dream-like trance. What was between her and this Luke person anyway? They certainly looked chummy. When someone nearby began to gossip, he wondered if he had asked the question out loud because the person was talking about Luke and Genevieve.

"Looks like Luke and Genevieve are back on," the woman said to her friend.

The woman shook her head with a smile. "I hope it works out this time."

"Think he'll propose again?"

The other woman shrugged. "I hope so. If he does, she'd better say yes. A man like Luke is too good a catch to wait forever."

"They sure look happy and in love tonight," the first woman declared.

Darcy once again focused on the couple in question. Luke looked at Genevieve like he was seeing what Darcy was seeing, and Darcy's fists tightened in response. He searched Genevieve's face to try and read the way she was looking at Luke. She must have sensed his intense scrutiny because she turned to look at him in surprise, stopping short on the dance floor so she stumbled forward a step. Their eyes caught and held. She looked at him as intently as he looked at her. When he began to hope, she tore her eyes away, fastening them instead on Luke, and then she smiled.

Too late, the torturous words began to echo once again in Darcy's mind. And this time he believed them.

CHAPTER 16

*D*arcy was on a date when the call came. He blamed Genevieve for the bad direction his date was already headed, not only because he was thinking about her—as he had been constantly since he left Jo's farm—but also because her prediction about Vivian had come true.

The week after he left the farm—three months ago—Darcy had gone to Virginia as planned. The farther he drove from Kentucky, the better he had felt. Maybe his time there had been an aberration. Maybe because he was out of his element, the experience with Genevieve had seemed more intense than it actually was. After all, it had been two weeks. How was it possible to feel something so deep for someone he barely knew? All of the things he had originally told himself about her came to the forefront of his mind then. She was too short for him. They would look ridiculous together. She knew nothing about horses. But that was it; that was all he could come up with.

Instead his mind started to go in the opposite direction, listing all the things he liked about her. Outside of his brothers she was the closest thing he had to a best friend. She was the best, most loving, most fun, smartest person he knew. Her ability to enjoy life was…

He had cut himself off then, determined to put her from his mind. For a few hours, it had worked. Vivian was as lovely as he remembered. Tall and stacked, she could have been a contender for Miss America, and she knew as much about horses as he did. Her parents' property was vast and beautiful. Her horses were sublime. The meal they shared with her family was pleasant. And he was bored out of his mind.

He waited with baited breath for her to say something funny or witty or smart or even inappropriate, but it was as if she was reading from a script she had received in finishing school. One thing was for certain, he couldn't stay there all week. He would lose his mind.

So after two days he made his excuses and returned to Kentucky. Not that his excuses weren't legitimate. He had been away from his job for a long time, and work was piling up in Lexington. Vivian had been very understanding when he told her goodbye, smiling vacantly and nodding her head as she stood in front of him, waiting for his kiss. And he had kissed her, if for no other reason than to assure himself that the kiss with Genevieve had been a fluke. But the kiss with Vivian was nothing like the kiss with Genevieve had been. Vivian's lips were as bland as the rest of her, though they were also as pretty.

But then the farther he drove from Virginia, the more he convinced himself that things with Vivian hadn't gone as bad as he thought they had. Maybe he hadn't been fair to her. Maybe he hadn't given her enough of a chance. After all, he was very confused right now. Maybe what he needed was another date.

And so they had met in the middle, three hours from each of them, but the distance only served to remind him of how far his Aunt Jo lived, of how far Genevieve was from him. The second date with Vivian had gone even worse than the first. But he had still dutifully kissed her goodbye. Then, once again feeling guilty for giving her only half his attention, he had asked her out again.

This time she was in Lexington and staying with his family for the night. Darcy was determined to put maximum effort into the date. He took her to the best restaurant in Lexington and they were going to see a play later. The evening was so fancy, in fact, that he was wearing a tuxedo and Vivian was wearing an evening gown. She looked stunning, like someone who had fallen from a fashion magazine. Darcy tried, really tried, to keep his thoughts focused on her. If his mind began to travel three hours away and think about a tiny little woman with choppy hair, he studiously reeled his thoughts back in.

But when his phone rang and he saw it was from his Aunt Jo, he practically pounced on the phone in his haste to answer.

"Hello," he said, drawing angry looks from other diners in the restaurant. He held up a finger to Vivian, indicating he would be right back. With an apologetic smile he excused himself and walked outside.

"Darcy." It was Genevieve, and she was crying.

"What is it, sweetheart?" he asked gently, already knowing and dreading what the answer would be.

"Darcy, Jo's gone," she said, or at least that's what he thought she said. It was difficult to tell between her weeping. "I need you. Can you come here?"

He was halfway to his SUV before she finished the sentence, and not until he arrived home did he remember he had left Vivian at the restaurant.

He didn't go back for her. He sent Everett, along with his apologies, knowing it was undoubtedly the end of his fledgling relationship with Vivian. He tried to feel bad about that, but he couldn't. All he could focus on was the fact that Genevieve needed him, and he had to go to her as soon as possible.

After landing at home to deliver the bad news to his family and dispatching Everett to retrieve Vivian, he hastily threw a bag together and was on his way again. Even though he made record time, it was still late when he arrived at Jo's farm. And even though he was late, all the lights were on and the driveway was lined with cars.

Inside the house, the atmosphere was more like a party as neighbors and friends circulated, talking and eating. Darcy swerved through the house, hunting for Genevieve. He saw Luke, but Genevieve was nowhere nearby. On a hunch, he left the house again and headed for the stable. He heard her before he saw her, though she tried to stifle her sobs.

When he reached Lou's stall, his heart clenched at the sight of Genevieve sitting down, the foal's head resting in her lap like a dog. She looked up at Darcy's approach, only hesitating a second before opening her arms to him. He knelt and picked her up, settling her in his lap as he sat on the soft straw.

"There now," he said, his voice breaking with emotion of his own. After that, he didn't try to speak. He simply held her, allowing her tears to soak his shirt while her body shook with unbearable grief. At last her crying came to an end. She sagged limply in his arms, totally drained of all emotion.

"What happened?" he asked at last.

"I've been living here the last week," she said. "I knew it was near the end, even if she wouldn't admit it. It was like watching a clock slowly wind down. I begged her to let me take her to the hospital or to call your parents, but she said she wanted to die at home, and she didn't want a lot of people around. Just me." She choked out the words and shuddered, repressing more tears.

"She loved you as if you were her own," Darcy said, smoothing his hand up and down her arm.

"I loved her," she said vehemently. "She was my family, my only family."

Darcy gave her a gentle squeeze, wanting to tell her she wasn't alone, but he couldn't. True to his promise, he had visited Jo every couple of weeks since he left, but Genevieve had always been noticeably absent. He had the feeling that she would arrive, see his SUV in the driveway, and go away again.

"Everyone is here, and they're so nice," Genevieve continued. "But all I want is to be alone with my grief."

"I can go," Darcy said.

"I didn't mean you," she admitted softly, gathering his shirt in her fist and holding on tight, as if to keep him anchored in position.

"Then I'll stay," he assured her, covering her ear with his hand and pressing her comfortingly closer to his chest. He noted as he held her that she felt a little more solid. As he looked down, inspecting her in the semi-darkness of the barn, he thought maybe she had gained a good ten pounds and he smiled, hoping it meant she was on the mend. She tipped her face up to study him as he studied her, and with a jolt he realized she had eyelashes and eyebrows again. He hadn't noticed the lack of them before, but he had understood that something was off about her face. Now that they were back, they framed her eyes, highlighting the blue depths. Her lashes were long and pretty, fanning her cheeks which were fuller and rosier. He wanted to tell her how pretty she was, but not only was it the wrong moment in the middle of her grief, it would also serve to remind her how he had failed to find her pretty before when she had needed him the most.

Instead he traced her face with his index finger, over and over again until her eyes drifted shut and she fell asleep. He wondered if she had slept at all since she'd arrived to care for Jo. It had to have been an exhausting and draining process, not only physically but emotionally as she watched one she loved slowly slip away. He wished she had defied Jo's wishes and called him anyway, but maybe she hadn't wanted to. The thought that she might not have wanted to was painful, so he refused to dwell on it. She had called him after the fact, and that was what mattered.

He reached for a clean horse blanket, glad the barn was heated. It was November, and the weather was still comfortable, but Genevieve always ran cold. Even now in his arms, she shivered, though Darcy wasn't sure if it was from cold or emotion. He would wait until the crowd left the house, and then he would carry her inside and put her to bed. That was his intention, but as the warmth of the blanket settled over him, his blinks became longer until he eventually fell asleep.

CHAPTER 17

*W*hen he woke, Genevieve was staring at him. "You still snore," she whispered.

He looked up. "The rafters are still intact."

"Barely," she said.

He shifted, resettling her more comfortably in his embrace. She snuggled closer, burrowing, as he tucked the blanket more securely around them. "You're wearing a tuxedo," she noted absently.

"I was on a date," he announced.

"How did it go?" she asked, a smile hinting at the corners of her mouth.

"I forgot her and left her sitting in the restaurant. I sent Everett back for her."

"I'm sorry," she said.

"I'm not," he replied, giving her a squeeze. "Missed you, Genevieve."

She didn't reply at first, absently smoothing her hand over his chest until at last she spoke. "Darcy."

"Hmm."

She tipped her face up again. "I never realized how nice it is to be held by someone so much larger."

"I'm rather enjoying it myself," he said, smiling. He grasped her chin between his thumb and index finger, dipping his head to meet hers when suddenly she was out of his embrace and a few feet away.

"I can't," she said, her voice unsteady. "I can't do this right now." She turned and sprinted toward the house, tripping on the blanket that was still draped around her shoulders.

Darcy sat in the barn for a long time, until the sound of a couple of cars alerted him to the fact that his family had arrived. He stood, shaking the hay from his tuxedo, and headed toward the house. Genevieve was emerging from her room when the Honeywells trooped onto the porch, nine of them including Allie and Haley.

Genevieve opened the door with a pensive smile until Grant rushed forward and picked her up in a bear hug. "Genevieve, is that you, sugar? I nearly didn't recognize you."

"You too, Grant. Have you shrunk? I remember you being taller somehow," Genevieve replied, craning her neck to look up at him as the family chuckled. Grant stood back, searching for Darcy. His eyes settled on Darcy's rumpled tuxedo questioningly before he stood back so Darcy could make the introductions.

Darcy stepped forward and introduced Genevieve to his parents, Haley, and Allie, noting as he did so the changes in Genevieve. In the daylight, they were more apparent. She had filled out and, though she was still a bit thin, she looked healthy. Her hair was thicker, shinier, and longer. She looked like a different person but, to Darcy's confusion, he found that he missed the way she looked before. Why had he longed for her to look different only to now want her to return to the way she had been? He didn't understand himself at all lately. He wanted to put an encouraging arm around her as she was faced with so many of his relatives, but he realized Genevieve had never needed support where meeting people was a factor, and today was no different. She easily charmed his parents, teased his brothers, asked after Allie's wellbeing without insulting her burgeoning belly, and inquired about Haley's wedding plans—seemingly all in the same breath.

"I've been staying here the last couple of weeks with Jo," Genevieve explained, moving aside to allow the family entrance. "Normally I rent a house in town."

"We're so thankful you were able to be here with Jo, dear," Darcy's mother said. "Darcy has told us what a special relationship you and she had."

Genevieve teared up, but didn't cry. "I'll gather my things and clear out so y'all will have more room," Genevieve said.

"Nonsense," Darcy's father said. "We rented a bed and breakfast in town, though one of the boys will have to stay here to look after the horses." His eyes, along with everyone else's, swiveled to Darcy and lingered, waiting for him to speak up.

"I'll stay," he said, trying not to frown at Genevieve's apparent discomfort with the situation.

They transitioned into the kitchen where Genevieve and Darcy's mom began pouring glasses of iced tea while his father and brothers discussed funeral arrangements. Jo had been very specific with Darcy during recent visits, so everyone knew exactly what she wanted to happen. Breaking with tradition, she preferred to be buried locally instead of the family plot in Silver Springs. The only thing she hadn't prearranged was a grave marker, and that was the current topic of debate.

Darcy watched Genevieve as she stood at the sink, her back to the room, and studiously scrubbed at an invisible spot on the faucet.

"What do you think, Genevieve?" he asked.

She jumped and turned, dropping the sponge. "I'm sorry, what?"

"What type of gravestone do you think Aunt Jo would prefer?"

Genevieve cleared her throat. "Something plain and simple. She wouldn't like anything fussy." She tried unsuccessfully to blink away the tears that were leaking over her lashes. Darcy motioned her forward and she hesitantly edged toward him until she was close enough to reach, then he put his arm around her waist, pulling her close so she was standing beside his chair, his arm still circling her. Tentatively, she rested her hand on his shoulder and squeezed, and they shared a smile.

But almost as soon as things began looking up, they came crashing back down again. The doorbell rang. Haley answered and returned to the kitchen followed by Luke. He stood at the edge of the kitchen and scanned the group of Honeywells until his eyes rested on Genevieve, who had moved away from Darcy when the doorbell rang. Genevieve introduced him to the room at large, and he nodded politely.

"I don't mean to intrude. I stopped by to check on Genevieve."

Genevieve scurried toward him and excused them as they went into the other room. Darcy wanted to call her back, but what could he say? He had no rights where she was concerned. As far as he knew, they might be dating again. Then a cold sweat broke out on his forehead. What if they were engaged? What if Luke had proposed and Genevieve had accepted? What would Darcy do then?

He realized then that, not only was his entire family staring at him, but he was also gripping the edge of his seat as he leaned intently toward the living room. He cleared his throat, dropping his eyes to the table while consciously relaxing his grip on the chair and conversation began to flow again.

From that moment on, Darcy couldn't seem to grab a minute alone with Genevieve. Not only because she busily flitted from one task to another—including preparing lunch and supper for his entire family —but because she was obviously avoiding him. He thought they would have plenty of time to talk after his family retired to the bed and breakfast where they were staying, but as soon as they headed toward the door, Genevieve did, too, bag in hand.

"Would you mind dropping me at my house?" she asked Grant.

He froze and looked uncertainly at Darcy, as did everyone else. "Why are you going home?" Darcy asked.

"I haven't been there in almost two weeks. I really need to check on a few things," she replied, though she didn't look directly at him when she spoke.

Darcy sighed, biting back his frustration. What could he do? Demand she stay with him so they could talk? He had higher hopes for the next day, but it was also the viewing and funeral, so it wouldn't exactly be ideal for conversation.

In the morning he spent a long time with the horses. Besides

Genevieve and the kids, the horses had been the thing his Aunt Jo liked the best. Darcy felt like he was saying his own farewell to her as he fed and watered them. Maybe it was his imagination, but they all seemed subdued this morning, as if they sensed the loss of their master. Darcy was thankful he'd really gotten to know his aunt these last few months. Without Genevieve, he might have gone on believing his aunt was a hard-hearted, lonely recluse. Now he knew that her abrupt nature was a cover for a soft, generous, and loving heart, one that she had shared with everyone in her community.

He met up with his family for breakfast, where they were the center of attention as people talked and whispered about them, pointing behind their hands. Darcy was usually oblivious to such things, but today it amused him because he knew people were comparing them to Jo and wondering if they were worthy to be her relatives. He wished for Genevieve in a way that left a dull ache in his chest. Maybe it was the grief, or maybe it was because he had missed her so much the last few months. Whatever the reason, he hadn't been able to take his eyes off her the previous day as she had flitted around the house, serving everyone but herself, even in the midst of her grief.

She was waiting at the church when they arrived. She had been in the chapel with the coffin, saying her final goodbyes. When the family arrived, she looked guilty, as if she had been trespassing, but no one minded her presence. They formed a receiving line, and Darcy realized she was nowhere in sight. He tracked her down in the church's kitchen where she was helping with the funeral lunch.

"What are you doing?" he said, startling her along with all the other women in the room who looked up at him in surprise.

"Working," she replied.

"Well stop it and come here," he commanded, holding out his hand to her. "I need you."

She took it tentatively, not understanding what he wanted of her until they reached the receiving line, and then she tried to pluck her hand free. "This isn't right, Darcy, I'm not family. I shouldn't be here."

Instead of trying to tell her that she had more right than anyone to be there, he tried another tack. "You know all these people and we don't. It would be nice if you made the introductions for us."

"Okay," she said, relieved to have a task to perform. He positioned her between himself and his parents and she began the introductions, not merely telling them people's names, but also relating their connection to Jo and occasionally adding an anecdote as she thought of one. From there, people began to add their own stories about Jo, stories of how she had bought them food or paid for their utilities when they were out of work, of how she had bought braces for one family's child whose teeth were so bad she was in danger of losing them, of how she had bought a car for another family, trying to remain anonymous, though everyone knew it was her because no one else in town could afford it.

As the stories wore on, Genevieve began to cry, but then so did everyone else. The tears weren't from sadness, though. They were a celebration of the generous life that had passed, and maybe a little grief that they hadn't known her better.

Luke arrived and went through the receiving line. He shook Darcy's hand, though he proffered no words of condolence and Darcy didn't think it was his imagination that the handshake was overly tight. Transversely, he hugged Genevieve tightly, kissing her cheek and whispering in her ear. "I'm here for you, sweetheart."

"What's with you two?" Darcy whispered when he moved on, but Genevieve's only response was to narrow her eyes and shake her head at him.

Was she telling him it was none of his business? Or was she saying it was the wrong time to ask such a question. With chagrin, Darcy realized both things were true.

After seemingly everyone in town had snaked through the receiving line and spoken a word about Jo, it was time for the funeral. The pastor added his own list of stories about Jo, making the day feel like even more of a celebration of her life, and then everyone went to the cemetery for the graveside service.

Darcy kept his arm around Genevieve who actually seemed

grateful of the support as she wept copiously. He kept his arm around her, herding her toward his SUV where they were finally alone.

"Where are we going?" she asked when she realized it wasn't back to the farm.

"I need to talk to you," he said. "It's important."

"Darcy…" she began, but he interrupted.

"It's important, Genevieve. It's business."

That intrigued her enough to keep still until he arrived at the park where he had watched her dance with Luke. For once she stayed in the car until he came for her, but he thought it was because she was too tired and dazed with grief to move. They walked to the gazebo and sat down. A cold wind rattled through the open space, and she shivered. Darcy took off his jacket and draped it over her, cinching it close around her middle.

"What's this about, Darcy?" she asked, sounding tired.

"I did a lot of talking with Jo and my family, especially Brent," he said. Realizing that last part meant nothing to her, he went on to explain. "Brent is our family lawyer. Anyway, it was important to Jo both that her legacy continues and that you are taken care of. In that vein, we've drawn up a trust for her estate, and we're starting a charity foundation that you are now in charge of. Your duties will be similar to what they are now, only you'll live in her house and have the money at your disposal to make the program grow. You're getting a raise, a big one. Oh, and we bought you a van. It'll be here tomorrow. We'll hire someone to look after the horses and grounds as soon as we can find someone suitable who can work on a fulltime basis."

If the expression on her face was any indication, she was stunned. "Darcy, I…I don't know what to say except thank you." She blinked a few more times in confusion and then she gave him the radiant smile he hadn't seen since Jo's death. "What am I doing? Thank you!" She threw her arms around him, hugging tightly. He returned her embrace, practically swallowing her in his arms. The hug lengthened beyond what was appropriate for simple gratitude. His hand slid up and down her back, caressing, and her arms tightened on his neck before he eased her away, aiming for her lips.

Genevieve held up a hand and backed away. "No," she said, her tone resolved yet tinged with sadness.

Darcy opened his eyes and looked at her. "I blew my chance with you, huh?" he asked.

"I'm afraid so, but we can still be friends," she said.

"Okay," he said, trying not to sound as dismal as he felt. "Friends." He bypassed her lips and kissed her cheek. "Let's get you home. It's freezing."

They walked to his car in silence. Genevieve's head was full of new information, but Darcy's head was full of the same old refrain. *Too late; it's too late.*

CHAPTER 18

*D*arcy was a half an hour from home when he realized he was in love with Genevieve.

He had no idea what sparked the thought, but it rose up to slap him in the face, jolting him so that he had to swerve and pull off the side of the road, bending over the steering wheel to try and catch a breath. Once the initial shock wore off, he was angry with himself. Of course he was in love with her. How could he not have known that already? He thought of her constantly, longed for her with a physical ache that never went away, and cared about every aspect of her life.

He turned his head to the side, resting his cheek on the steering wheel. Maybe there was something seriously wrong with him. How else to explain his complete lack of awareness about the world around him? Did his brothers have this problem, too? Had Brent and Corliss had this much trouble falling in love?

He sat up, shaking off his brief moment of melancholy. Now that he had realized he was in love with Genevieve, there was only one thing to do about it: he was going to go and get her. And, being a Honeywell, he didn't care that there were obstacles in his path. He would simply bulldoze over them until he achieved his goal.

Still, the first obstacle was the most difficult because it was his own family. His parents had never said he owed them anything, but he felt he did. He didn't like leaving them high and dry without their own personal veterinarian. They had invested a lot not only in his education, but also in him as a person, and he wanted to repay that in any way he could. But when he said as much to his father an hour later, his father waved him dismissively away.

"Darcy, you're our son before you're our vet. Veterinarians are a dime a dozen, but we only have four other sons." His father had grinned at him before continuing. "Mom and I love you, and we want what's best for you. We'll miss you, but it's important for you to do what's best for you and Genevieve. Sometimes leaving is what's best. Besides, you'll only be a few hours away. You can slip over occasionally when there's a problem."

Darcy laughed because his business-minded father might talk a good game about being supportive, but Darcy knew he still had every intention of keeping him as his primary veterinarian.

"I'll come whenever you need me, Dad. And if things work out the way I plan, then we'll be busy in the summer and slower in the winter. We could split our time between the two places so I can still help oversee the herd here."

"Whatever works best for you," his father said, but by the hopeful light in his eyes, Darcy knew he was hoping he would still be able to get a few months of free veterinary care per year.

They hugged, Darcy packed, said goodbye to his brothers and mother, and then he was driving back toward Appalachia and Genevieve.

G enevieve was happily oblivious as she once again settled into Jo's house. She felt lonely without Jo's gentle presence, and she found herself talking to her almost constantly throughout the day.

"I think you were right about the camp idea, Jo," Genevieve said as she prepared lunch for herself. "That's the best way to cast a wider net over the area. It's going to take a while until I become more familiar with the legalities of my new job, but I'll have all winter to plan." She bit her lip. "Maybe we can expand the housing to include a couple of cabins with bunk beds."

A knock on the door interrupted her thoughts. Thinking it must be Luke, she answered with a smile that soon faded as she took in Darcy, all 6'10" of him, as he lounged in the doorway, a garment bag thrown carelessly over his shoulder.

"Darcy," she said.

"Hey, Genevieve," he answered. Not waiting for an invitation, he shouldered his way inside and dropped his bag.

"What are you doing here?" she asked.

"I was on my way home, and I decided I love you. And since you've already refused two very nice proposals from other men, I decided I'm simply going to tell you that you're going to marry me. Oh, and as of now I live here and we're partners in the charity." He craned his neck around the kitchen doorway. "Are you eating lunch? I'm starved."

"Wait, what?" she said.

He turned to look at her. "Which part?"

"All of it."

"I'm in love with you and we're getting married," he said.

"And what was the part about the charity?"

"We'll be running it together, obviously, though I still might hang out my shingle and do some veterinary work on the side. Maybe I'll do it for free. I'm sure this area could use some free veterinary care. Is there enough food in the house, or do we need to go to the store?"

"No."

"No we don't need to go to the store?"

"Stop talking about the store and food," she yelled. "We're talking about my life here, and you are not taking it over, Darcy Honeywell."

He rolled his eyes. "Obviously not, Genevieve. I'm trying to tell you we're going to share it. You know, partners."

"I don't want a partner," she said, so angry she couldn't see straight.

"Sure you do," he answered.

"No I don't," she said, clenching her hands into fists and jamming them to her sides. "And I don't want a husband. I'm not marrying you."

"Okay," he said.

"Okay?" she asked.

"Sure," he said with an easy smile. He began advancing on her then. She backed up until she bumped into the wall, but he didn't stop until he reached her. Then he slipped his arms around her and spoke. "You don't have to marry me. I can't make you do that. But I do control your endowment so, technically speaking, I'm your boss. You have to accept me as your business partner. We'll live here, work together every day, and we'll keep things strictly professional." He leaned down and scraped his teeth gently over a sensitive spot on her neck.

Genevieve closed her eyes and leaned her head against the wall. She felt like she was sinking, as if an actual weight was physically pulling her toward him. Mustering her last ounce of self-preservation, she opened her eyes and shoved at his chest.

"No," she said.

"No?" he asked.

"You didn't want me, Darcy. Did you know I have never suffered from low self-esteem until I met you? Even though I've never put much faith in outward appearances, I knew I was pretty. Then I lost my hair, my eyelashes, my complexion, my figure, everything, and I tried to tell myself that it didn't matter, that I was still beautiful. But I met you, and I knew you thought otherwise. You made me feel bad about myself for the first time in my life. I don't think I can ever forgive you for that. And I won't stay here and be a part of your scheme. You can't walk in here and take over a charity that I started, something I've given my life to, and make it your own."

"I'm not trying to make it my own. I'm trying to help you. I'll be in charge of the grounds, horses, and money. You can still be in charge of the kids. When you think about it, having me involved will be a huge plus for you. You can concentrate on what you want and leave the details to me."

"I don't want to leave the details to you,"

He shrugged as if to say there was nothing to do about it.

Genevieve furiously searched her mind until at last she knew what she needed to do. "I quit," she said, throwing out the words like a challenge.

"I'll miss you. You won't be easy to replace."

She growled in frustration and picked up the keys from the counter. "I'm moving back home."

He plucked the keys from her fingers. "The van is for employees only. Sorry."

"Then I'll walk home," she said tightly between gritted teeth.

"I'll give you a ride," he said, smiling. He kept the same stupid smile as he walked down the hall, helped her pack, and drove her home.

CHAPTER 19

For three days, Genevieve alternately seethed and felt sorry for herself. It was the first time since her childhood that she had indulged in self pity, and she blamed Darcy for that, too. What was it about the man that broke her carefully constructed emotional shield? And why did she find herself wanting to throttle him one minute and kiss him the next? He drove her absolutely crazy and she was torn between wanting to run away forever and run back up the mountain to his waiting arms.

It didn't help matters that she had no phone, no car, and no money. When she thought of how he had given her the charity and then taken it away again in a matter of two days, she became angry with him all over again. How dare he?

When the authoritative knock sounded on her door, she knew it was him. Who else knocked as if he owned the place? She debated not answering, but she had never been petty, and she wouldn't allow Darcy to make her immature in addition to everything else she had become.

"Yes?" she said, satisfied with the frosty coolness of her tone. For all the warmth she infused, he might have been a stranger selling encyclopedias.

"Allie's in labor. Want to come with me? I'll let you hold the baby." He wagged his eyebrows at her.

Genevieve wanted to remain resolute, she really did, but the inducement of a newborn was too much and he knew it, the cad. "All right," she said grudgingly.

"Pack for a week," he called before she slammed the door in his face. He remained waiting on her doorstep while she hastily threw together an assortment of clothes. She could protest staying a week, but it wouldn't do any good. If Darcy said they were going for a week, then they were going for a week.

"Control freak," she muttered under her breath as she stuffed a handful of underpants in her bag. "I must be crazy."

"Still mad, huh?" Darcy asked as they began their journey, breaking the heavy silence between them.

"Furious," Genevieve replied. To her further irritation, he smiled. "Why is that good news?"

"Because it means you're passionate and we have good chemistry."

"It's not passion, Darcy, it's anger," she insisted. Though, if she were being honest, she would admit she was as angry with herself as she was with him. For as long as she could remember, she had self-righteously declared the shallowness of judging a man on looks, status, or money, proclaiming that character was the only thing that counted. And what did she do? She fell in love with a gorgeous, rich doctor who, somewhere in his family's impressive lineage, was a cousin to George Washington, who had more money than some small countries. And, to top it all off, he was as shallow as a drop of water. Genevieve wasn't angry; she was incensed.

They reached the hospital and Darcy lifted her from the SUV, suspending her in midair a few beats so they were eye level.

"Pretty," he said, smiling. His gaze dropped to her lips, and she knew he wanted to kiss her. She wanted that, too, though she would never admit it.

"Sure, you think that *now*," she said.

He shook his head. "I thought it before. Maybe not at first, but I got there eventually. And you had it backwards, you know." He set her on the ground and took her hand.

She hated to ask, but she was too curious. "What are you talking about?"

"The story, beauty and the beast. You were never the beast; you were always the beauty. I was the beast—selfish and clueless, I didn't understand what you meant about true beauty until I saw it in you."

His words had a softening effect, but she steeled herself against them, not sure if she could trust him. After all, he was saying all this now when she was herself again. But his feelings could change if she changed, too. "You're too tall for me. We look ridiculous together."

"No argument there," he said. "But do you really care how we look? Holding you feels perfect."

"Dancing won't," she said.

He smiled down at her. "You're being uncharacteristically pessimistic."

"It's my turn," she said, though it was difficult to maintain her bad mood in the excitement of the hospital waiting room. All the Honeywells were there, including some Genevieve had never met before.

"Genevieve, this is my sister Ivy, her daughter, Jess, and her husband. We call him the Yankee."

"Coy," the husband volunteered with a friendly handshake. He grasped Genevieve's left hand and inspected it. "No ring, number three?" he asked Darcy.

"I'm working on it," Darcy said tightly.

"Don't give in too easily, Genevieve," Coy said.

"I have no plans to give in at all," Genevieve replied.

"You'll give in," Coy said resignedly. "I can only hope you make him properly miserable in the process." Coy smiled, dimpling, as Darcy dragged her away.

"Let's talk to Haley," Darcy said. "She's better company. You're on my list," he added to his brother-in-law.

"Nothing new there," Coy said easily, returning his attention to his daughter.

They sat next to Haley who bestowed them with a beaming smile.

"I apologize, but I've lost track of your wedding date," Genevieve said. "Are you married now?"

"In three days," Haley replied. "That's why Coy and Ivy are here. It's a pleasant coincidence that they were able to make it for the baby's birth, too. You're coming to the wedding, aren't you?" She turned hopeful eyes on Genevieve.

"Of course she is," Darcy answered for her.

"I don't have a dress," Genevieve said helplessly, shooting sparks at Darcy. Why hadn't he told her there was going to be a wedding?

"Ivy, Genevieve needs a dress for the wedding," Darcy announced.

Ivy scanned Genevieve who resisted the urge to run a comb through her hair and apply makeup. Something about Ivy's cool beauty was intimidating, even though she seemed perfectly sweet.

"Size zero petite?" Ivy guessed.

"Yes, but..." Genevieve started, but Ivy ignored her, nodding at Darcy.

"No problem," she said.

"See? Problem solved," Darcy said.

"But..." Genevieve tried, but he railroaded her again.

"You wouldn't want to insult my family by refusing to attend a wedding while you're a guest in their house, would you?" Darcy asked.

"Of course not, but..."

"And you couldn't leave me without a date. What would people say if I showed up without my fiancée?"

"You don't have a fiancée," she said, grasping the hair at her temples in a desperate attempt to keep her sanity.

"Watching a Honeywell male in action is everything I thought it would be and more," Coy said. "I feel like I need popcorn to enhance my enjoyment of the show."

"It gets better," Haley said sympathetically to Genevieve. "After the pursuit is over, they really do turn out to be a good choice."

Before Genevieve could find a reply to that, Corliss emerged wearing too-small scrubs that only reached mid thigh. He would have looked comical if not for the blissful expression on his face.

"She's here; she's perfect; she's nine pounds and Allie hates me," he announced.

The family stood up to give hugs and congratulations before following him to the nursery viewing area to watch the baby be cleaned, weighed, and measured. Genevieve tried to hang back, but Darcy wouldn't allow it.

"You're family now, sweetheart. Might as well start acting like it."

Protesting was futile, and she didn't want to; she was dying to see the newest addition. When they reached the window, Corliss pointed, but there was no need. Everyone could spot the newest Honeywell, not only because she was the largest baby in the nursery—so tall she almost reached the end of her crib—but she also had a thatch of black hair on top, as thick and dark as Corliss or any of his brothers.

"What's her name?" Genevieve asked Darcy. Since no one else had bothered to ask, she figured they already knew it.

"Keeley, of course," Darcy answered

"Why of course?" she asked.

"Because it starts with a K. We have an alphabetical theme going. Ivy was the last one of us, then her baby is Jess. Now we have Keeley. Ivy's next baby will begin with an L and then it will probably be Brent's turn. By the time it gets to us, we might have to start over with the A's."

She didn't bother to remind him that they weren't, in fact, engaged. His words caused a painful yearning in her chest that was hard to ignore. Instead she concentrated on the giant newborn in its crib, sighing dreamily when she opened her perfect mouth and yawned. Darcy noticed. He wrapped his arms around her and pulled her back slightly so she rested against his chest.

"Marry me, Genevieve, and I'll give you a dozen of those," he whispered.

"That's the best offer I've had yet," she said, trying and failing not to sound wistful. "Do you think we could actually have kids together?" she added, too curious to be embarrassed.

"I'm positive," he said.

Genevieve was still dubious, thinking a nine pound baby might kill her.

"Allie's not tall," he said, reading her mind. "She's only 5'5", and Ivy's baby only weighed six pounds. Babies are a mixed bag; you never know what you'll get."

She tried not to let his words affect her, but it was impossible, especially when the baby was finally prepped and able to be passed around the family. When it was Genevieve's turn, she felt her heart turning somersaults as she looked at the beautiful little girl. She was so large, she required two arms, at least for Genevieve, but she didn't mind. She stared at her for a long time, inhaling her new baby smell and memorizing her perfect face. If she knew Allie at all, she would volunteer to watch the baby any time Allie needed sleep. But she didn't know her, and her mother, Sandy, was nearby, providing all the relief the new mother would need. With a heavy heart, Genevieve handed Keeley over to the next Honeywell in line, turning away to hide the yearning in her expression.

"You must be tired," Darcy said gently. "Let's go home."

Home. What did that word mean to her? Right now it meant her tiny rental house where she had never felt comfortable or at peace. She hadn't known the security of a real home since her parents died. As much as she had tried to put down roots in the community, the only one that had stuck was Jo, and now Jo was gone.

Darcy held her hand on the way to his car, and she let him. He helped her into the truck, and she let him do that, too. She also didn't protest when he lifted her back down and kissed her. This kiss matched the intensity of the one they'd shared in Jo's barn, but it didn't feel like enough for Genevieve; she wanted more.

It was Darcy who broke away, resting his forehead on the side of his tall SUV and sucking oxygen. "Is that a yes?" he asked shakily.

Genevieve shook her head, still unable to speak.

He grinned. "All right, but so you know, I don't generally kiss women like that unless they're about to be my wife."

She smiled, not believing his lie for a second, and then to both their dismay, she burst into tears. He set her inside the vehicle again and slid in beside her, holding her close while she cried.

"What is it?" he asked, smoothing his hand comfortingly along her spine.

"I'm not sure I can ever have kids," she said. "I took so many drugs during chemotherapy, and…" She broke off, sobbing, but Darcy chuckled.

"Of course you can," he said confidently. "At least if you marry me, you can. I have no idea what your chances are with other men."

"What are you talking about?" she asked, swiping at her eyes.

"I'm talking about the fact that I'm a Honeywell. I told you we're fertile, and I wasn't exaggerating."

"What does your fertility have to do with me? *I'm* not a Honeywell."

"When you marry me you will be," he said.

"Darcy, it doesn't work that way," she said, becoming irritated now. How did he think she was going to absorb his fertility? By osmosis?

"Sure it does, at least in our family it does. I'm telling you it won't be a problem, but if you don't believe me I would be happy to prove it. Marry me, and I'll get you pregnant."

She laughed in the middle of a sob, knowing she looked and sounded like a mental patient. "That's the most unromantic thing anyone has ever said to me." Laughter won over crying and she swiped at her eyes again.

"I wasn't kidding."

"That's what makes it even worse," she said, holding her stomach because it hurt now from laughing so hard. He smiled as he watched her laugh, but soon her amusement faded away to be replaced by gravity once again.

"I can't get pregnant for a while," she said. "I need to make sure I'm really well first."

"What do you mean?" he asked, something like panic snaking around his heart.

"It means I could go out of remission. I'm not considered cured for five years."

"We'll wait. You'll only be thirty one. That's not so old."

An exasperated sigh slid between her teeth. "Stop talking like us getting married is a done deal." His tenacity was confusing her because she was beginning to think like him, talking as if they were already engaged.

"It is," Darcy replied.

"It is not. There's the small matter of me agreeing to marry you, which I haven't."

"You will," he said.

"What makes you so certain?" she asked.

"Because I can't live with any other alternative. By the way, if you're dating Luke, you should probably break up with him."

"Darcy," Genevieve said, grinding her palms into her eyes.

"When are you going to look at your ring?" he asked.

She removed her hands from her eyes and looked at him. "You already have a ring?"

"Who proposes without a ring? That's tacky."

"You didn't propose," she shouted, causing the sound to echo off the small space.

"I can change that right now," he said, beginning to withdraw something from his pocket. She grabbed his arm to stop him.

"No. Stop this. You are not proposing, and I am not accepting, we are not getting married, and that's that. Let's go home so I can try to get some sleep and forget everything for a few blissful hours."

Darcy smiled.

"What?" she snapped, already dreading the answer.

"You called the farm 'home.' You're already talking like a Honeywell."

Genevieve groaned, dropping her head into her hands once again.

CHAPTER 20

*S*leep worked to erase any vestiges of Genevieve's sadness, though she was still angry with Darcy, especially when he introduced her to people as his fiancée, which he did to everyone they met. After trying to tell people she wasn't, she realized there was no graceful way to undo his lie, so she simply went along with it, smiling demurely and saying a polite hello, all the while chalking up Darcy's offenses against him.

In the afternoon, he took her for a ride on one of his horses. Unlike with Sally, the gentle mare, this time he wanted to ride on one of his wicked-looking black stallions. If he had proposed putting her on one by herself, she might have objected, but since she knew he would be riding with her, she didn't much care which horse they took. Horses were all the same, weren't they?

Only it turned out they weren't. Sally was sweet and gentle and clomped along at an equally gentle pace. The stallion was strong, sleek, and fast. He didn't clomp; in fact Genevieve wasn't sure his feet actually touched the ground. He seemed to be gliding on air, so smooth was their ride. This time when they rode, Darcy wasn't content to keep his hands to himself. She remembered how he had briefly rested his fingers on her bony ribs at Jo's house. The sensation had lingered with her for the remainder of the day, despite her best efforts to ignore it. Now, however, they were sandwiched close together. His left hand remained stationary on her waist while his right hand explored practically everywhere else.

How was she supposed to maintain her anger with him when he kept smoothing aside her hair to kiss her neck? And there wasn't much she could do to stop him, trapped as she was on a horse that was taller than she was. Not that she actually tried very hard to get him to stop. But that was what she wanted. In principle.

A part of her, however, remained indignant that he was so happy to be touching her now that she had regained most of her figure. Before, when she had resembled a skeleton with skin, he had wanted nothing to do with her. She said as much to him, trying to regain some distance between them.

"That's not true," he said. "If you'll recall, I kept trying to touch you, but you told me to stop."

For a stunned second, she had no reply to that. She had told him to stop touching her, both because he had been a stranger and because she hadn't wanted him to notice how skinny she had become. Also there was the alarming sensation that his touch had caused, and Genevieve hadn't wanted to admit the attraction she felt for him. She still didn't.

"If I told you to stop now, would you listen?" she asked.

"You could try, but I don't think you really want me to stop touching you." Finished with one side of her neck, he began working on the other. "Do you?" he asked, his breath warm on her ear.

"Soon," she said unconvincingly, and they both laughed before Genevieve rolled her eyes. She was hopeless. There was a part of her, a not so small part, that wanted to give in, accept his proposal, and satisfy her roaring curiosity over the ring he had chosen for her. But there was still that small voice in the back of her head that held her back, the same one that reminded her of his rejection when she had been at her worst. How could she marry a man she couldn't depend on when times were hard? Darcy was being very attentive and solicitous now, but Genevieve was almost back to one hundred percent.

She still missed her long hair, but she still looked pretty good, much better than she had three months ago when she and Darcy first met. And it bothered her, really bothered her, that he hadn't been able to see past her outer shell during that horrible time.

Later that afternoon a package arrived for Darcy, and he carried it to the living room and Genevieve with a smug smile. He was waiting for her to ask what it was, but she wouldn't give him the satisfaction. Instead she concentrated on stacking blocks with baby Jess.

"Our tickets to the derby came," Darcy announced. Though he had said it casually, he still caught Genevieve's attention.

"The derby?" she repeated. "As in *the* derby?"

"There's a slight catch, though. I can't take you if we're not married. It's a new rule I have about never taking anyone but my wife to the derby."

"Oh, wow," Coy said, turning his attention from a game on television to observe Darcy and Genevieve. "I really need to start writing this stuff down."

"What a coincidence because I have a rule about never marrying anyone who tries to blackmail me into attending the derby with him," Genevieve said.

"That's a good one," Coy commented, searching the desk beside him for a pen.

"I guess I'll have to figure out something to do with these tickets," Darcy said, holding them aloft so Genevieve could see the tantalizing image of the horse on front.

"We'll take them," Coy volunteered.

"Hush, Yankee. Return your attention to your knitting competition," Darcy said, waving his hand toward the television without looking at Coy. "May is a long time away; plenty enough time to plan a wedding," he added to Genevieve.

"I'll keep that in mind should I meet someone I intend to marry."

On the couch, Coy snorted a laugh and turned it into a cough.

The next day was Brent and Haley's wedding. The house was a flurry of activity, which suited Genevieve fine because she found a lot of ways to keep busy. To her amusement, Haley had nothing to do with the planning of her wedding, leaving it instead to Brent and his brothers.

"They're freakishly good at planning a party," she explained to Genevieve as she and Ivy sat in the room, talking to her as she got ready. "Plus I don't really care. I simply want to be with Brent."

Genevieve smiled. "Darcy told me your story. It's all very romantic."

"It didn't feel like it at the time. I wanted to hit him in the head with a brick a lot of the time in the beginning."

"I know that feeling," Genevieve said. "It's weird because when Darcy and I were only friends, I had a lot of fun teasing him. I liked him. Then he decided we should get married, and it's like a switch was flipped or something. Now he's driving me crazy, and I feel like I'm drowning in the lake of Honeywell adoration."

"That's their way," Ivy said sagely. "There's no subtlety once their minds are made up. It used to apply to me, too. They decided as soon as I was born that I was going to go to the University of Kentucky, and they wouldn't hear of anything else for me. It was maddening. At least Brent and Corliss have backed off Coy a little bit; I have my sisters-in-law to thank for that." She beamed at Haley as she helped pin her veil in place.

Genevieve felt a twinge of envy, though she had no idea why. Was it because Ivy and Haley would be sisters now and Genevieve had always longed for a sister? Or was it because Haley looked so beautiful with her long honey-colored hair and Genevieve was still vainly missing her hair? Or maybe it was the happiness and contentment that oozed from both women. Whatever the reason, she didn't like it. She had made it a point to find contentment where she was, not longing for things she didn't have. As she was about to slip unnoticed from the room, Ivy caught her hand and pulled her back.

"Your turn, Genevieve."

"My turn?" Genevieve asked, stupidly thinking Ivy was talking about marriage. Her panic began to ebb, only to be replaced by sheer joy as Ivy opened the closet and produced a blue dress in exactly the shade and style Genevieve would have chosen if she had enough money to buy such a dress for herself. "Oh, Ivy, it's so pretty, but it's too much. I can't accept this."

"Sure you can, you'll be family soon enough," Ivy said then, noticing Genevieve's grim expression, hastily added, "I mean, working for the Honeywell foundation and everything. Consider it a signing bonus."

Though she knew it wasn't what Ivy had meant, Genevieve decided to let it slide. After all, it wasn't Darcy's sister Genevieve was irritated with; it was Darcy himself. "How did you know the perfect dress?" she asked, smoothing her fingers over the shiny material.

"Fashion is my thing, I suppose. I hope you don't mind that I chose it without consulting you. My sisters-in-law in Montana allow me to dress them like life-size Barbie dolls, and I guess I've gotten used to doing without asking."

"I love it," Genevieve repeated, knowing she never would have chosen something so stylish and expensive. Spending money on herself wasn't something that came easily for her.

Haley's mother bustled in and claimed her attention, so Ivy and Genevieve were given a reprieve from attending to the bride. Genevieve used that time to style her hair and apply her makeup before slipping on the pretty dress.

Ivy spirited Haley out the back exit while Genevieve prepared to go through the front where Darcy was waiting for her at the bottom of the stairs. She felt a little bridal herself as she descended the stairs. He turned and there was a breathless pause while their eyes caught and held and then he slowly scanned the rest of her, smiling at what he saw.

"If I tell you you're beautiful, will you get mad at me again?" he asked.

She stopped on the third to last step so they were almost the same height. "Yes."

"You're gorgeous." He tipped her chin up and bestowed a light kiss on her lips, rattling her senses despite the chasteness of his touch. "We should go," he said, smiling because she was still staring in befuddlement at nothing at all.

Genevieve snapped to attention and finished walking down the stairs, falling into step beside him. Darcy looked down and smiled.

"Are you wearing heels?"

"Yes—four inches. I think maybe your sister is trying to kill me."

"Or give you enough height so people won't ask if you're a dwarf," Darcy suggested.

"You're saying that because you know I can't retaliate in these heels."

"Retaliate, please," Darcy begged. "I'm willing to take whatever punishment you deem necessary." They reached his car and his smile faded. He caught her left hand and looked down. "Want to wear your ring today? It'll save a lot of questions."

"There won't be any questions if you don't introduce me as your fiancée," she said.

"But I'll be seeing all our friends and family today. I want them to know the woman I intend to marry." He rested his hands on her waist. "Give in and say yes, Genevieve. You know you want to."

With effort, she slowly shook her head. "No, Darcy. The answer is no. No I won't wear the ring, and no I won't marry you."

"Yet," he added.

She sighed, dropping her head on his chest with a thump. He kissed the top of her head, gave her waist a squeeze and lifted her gently into the truck, taking care to make sure all of her dress was gathered inside before he closed the door.

The wedding was breathtaking. Genevieve had the stray thought that the brothers should plan her wedding, and quickly forced the thought away before it could take root.

She wasn't marrying Darcy; she couldn't let his relentless pursuit mess with her head.

After the wedding came the pictures. If Genevieve had any idea of Darcy's intentions, she would have slipped away and waited at the reception. Instead she had lingered in the sanctuary, enjoying watching Haley and Brent pose. And then it was time for the family photos and Darcy was motioning to her. She looked behind her, expecting and hoping to find a long-lost sibling or cousin, but, no, he was pointing at her.

"Come on, Genevieve," he said.

Mortified, she shook her head and began slowly backing away, but the rest of the family chorused their assent to the plan.

"C'mon, Genevieve," everyone else began to yell, beckoning her forward with sweeping hand gestures.

"Don't make us come get you," Grant added, and that was the deciding factor. If there was anything more embarrassing than being in a family picture when she wasn't part of the family, it was being hunted down and carried into the picture by a wild pack of Honeywells.

Her cheeks were probably magenta as she slowly plodded up onto the stage, but no one seemed to think anything amiss as Darcy put his arm around her and drew her close in front of him. "Know what would make this picture even better? Your ring," he whispered, loudly enough for everyone in the room to hear. Coy snickered until Ivy elbowed him in the stomach. And Genevieve was pretty sure that when the photos were developed, the expression on her face would be closer to a snarl than a smile.

Despite the embarrassment during the photo session, Genevieve was able to relax and enjoy the reception, and then the dancing started. For a few minutes, she and Darcy sat on the sidelines, content to watch, and then he held out his hand to her.

"What's that for?" she asked, staring at his palm.

"Let's dance," he said.

"We can't dance together; we'll look ridiculous."

"C'mon," Darcy prodded. "It'll be good practice for our wedding. Who cares about the height difference?"

"Anyone with eyes," Genevieve muttered, but she extended her hand and allowed him to lead her to the dance floor. They began swaying slowly back and forth and, even with her heels, she barely reached his sternum.

"I feel like I should be dancing on your feet," Genevieve said.

"This isn't the right type of music for us," Darcy said. "Hold on." He left her and went to speak to the DJ who nodded and began searching through his music selection. When Darcy returned to Genevieve, swing music began to play.

"You swing dance?" she asked in surprise.

"You don't?" he said, equally as surprised.

"A little," she said, laughing as he grabbed her hand and spun her away from him. Genevieve hated to admit it, but Darcy was right; swing dance was the right music choice for them. When he was pushing her away from him and pulling her back, it didn't really matter that he was two feet taller. And, more than that, it was fun. They weren't the only ones who thought so because the dance floor quickly filled up.

By the end of the next few songs, Genevieve was exhausted, breathless, couldn't feel her toes, and couldn't stop laughing. The thing about Darcy was that he was *fun*. Luke had been sweet and romantic. He was a good and loyal friend, but he didn't make her laugh. Granted, Darcy made her so angry she wanted to scream sometimes, but he also made her scream with laughter. With Luke, she had known something was missing, but she hadn't known what. Now, with Darcy, the missing piece finally fell into place—she needed to be with a man who knew how to have fun.

The song switched to another slow number. Genevieve turned to go back to their table, but Darcy held her back.

"Where are you going? I'm not done with you yet," he said.

"I thought we weren't going to dance the slow ones," she said.

"I never said that. I said we're a better fit for the fast ones. I still want to dance with my girl." He pulled her close, holding her hand out to the side while his other hand settled on her back. "How about it, Genevieve, are you going to marry me today? The minister is still on standby."

She shook her head. "Not today, Darcy," she replied.

"That's not a no," he said.

"You don't listen when I tell you no. I thought I'd try something different."

"Different is good," he declared. He gave her hand a cajoling shake. "C'mon, you know I love you. And I know you love me."

"How do you know? I never said."

"A man knows when a woman loves him," he said.

She laughed "Darcy Honeywell, you wouldn't know if a woman loved you unless she was wearing a sandwich board that told you so. You're clueless."

"So do you?" he asked. His smug smile told her she had walked right into his trap.

"Am I wearing a sandwich board?" she asked.

"I don't know, let me see." He pulled her closer, running his hands up and down her spine. "I don't feel one, but these things can be tricky. Maybe I'd better look again."

She laughed again, wriggling away from him. "Stop it; you're causing a scandal."

"Sweetheart, the last wedding I attended with this group of people, I ended up in a fountain. Believe me when I tell you that touching a pretty girl is the least scandalous thing they've seen me do."

"Why did you jump in a fountain?" she asked.

"Because I was on fire," he said.

She blinked at him, trying to determine if he was serious, and realizing he probably was. "Why were you on fire?"

"Marry me and I'll tell you."

She shoved at his chest again to gain a little more room. "Darcy," she intoned.

"Fine, if you won't agree to marry me then at least answer one other question for me."

"What?" she asked, wary now.

"Why did you say no to Luke?"

She bit her lip, scanning the room for a rescue. "How did you know it was Luke who proposed?"

"Not important. Are you going to answer the question?"

She stared at his chest, nervously plucking at an invisible thread on his tuxedo. "Luke is everything I want in a man. He's kind, loving, gentle, humble, and he has a sterling character."

"Please tell me there's a but in there somewhere," Darcy said peevishly.

"But I didn't love him," she added softly.

He was quiet for so long that she looked up. His eyes caught hers and held, looking vulnerable for the first time since she'd known him. "Is that why you're saying no to me?"

As much as she didn't want to, she had to tell him the truth. "No, that's not why I'm saying no to you," she replied softly.

He smiled, a slow, intense smile that turned her insides to jelly. "Good," he said, and they finished their dance in silence.

CHAPTER 21

The family spent the next morning recovering, and then Darcy and Genevieve went home. Genevieve hated to admit it, but she had fallen in love with Darcy's family as much as she loved the man himself. After so many children, his parents had endless patience and were seemingly unflappable. Even when Grant flung out his hands to make a point and shattered a window, they didn't even look up from their respective newspapers. His brothers were downright fun. Maybe it was because of the way Jo had described them, but Genevieve saw them as they had been--sweet and energetic boys looking for any mischief they could get into.

Ivy and the two sisters-in-law were equally as sweet and longsuffering as the parents. Ivy had an air about her as if she were a prisoner who had been given a reprieve. She loved her brothers, but occasionally her glance would dart to her husband, Coy, to make sure he was real and still around. Genevieve hadn't gotten to know the sisters-in-law as well because Allie had just arrived home from the hospital with her baby, and Haley was star-struck in love with Brent and full of wedding plans. Even so, Genevieve thought she had met three women she liked and could become friends with.

"My family loves you," Darcy declared as they started to drive.

She would have told him the feeling was mutual, but she didn't want to put any more ideas in his head about their future. Instead she smiled and squeezed his hand, the one that was holding hers, before looking down at it in dismay. When had he taken her hand? Was touching him so natural now that she didn't realize she was doing it? Odd.

"Genevieve, we need to talk," Darcy said, sounding serious for the first time in a long time. "You can't quit the charity."

With a jolt, the reason Genevieve had been so angry with him rose to the forefront once again. "Darcy, you can't come in and take over."

"That was never my intent," he said. "I don't know anything about kids or therapy, but I do know about horses and business. And I want to be a part of what you're doing."

She bit her lip, considering. "All your brothers live with your parents."

He darted her a frowning glance, confused by the shift in conversation. "Yes."

"You're the only one who isn't there."

He paused. "Ivy's not there," he said at last.

"Yes, but it's different, isn't it? Ivy doesn't carry the weight of the Honeywell legacy the way you do."

"What's your point here, sweetheart?" he asked, not understanding what she was trying to say.

"I want to know why you're doing this, Darcy, and don't say it's because of me."

He drew in a breath and let it out slowly. "I can't differentiate what's about you and what's not. If we weren't getting married, would I have quit my job to help you with yours? Probably not. But I do know that those two weeks I spent with you and Jo affected me deeply. I started looking at my life, and I didn't like what I saw. I want to make a difference. I want my life to mean something more than helping a mare successfully foal."

"But that's important, too," Genevieve said. "Think how much it meant to Jo that you were able to save Lou and her foal. By taking care of animals, you make their owners happy. And animals are important, too. They deserve a good vet, and you're a good vet, Darcy."

"And then there's you," Darcy continued as if she hadn't spoken. "I want to be with you. I want to do what you're doing. This is where your heart is; it wouldn't be fair to ask you to give it up and move to Silver Springs with me." He brought her hand to his lips and kissed it.

"Darcy, that's really sweet, but you can't give up your life for me."

"Yes I can," he insisted. "Besides, I had some ideas that might give us the best of both worlds."

"What sort of ideas?" she asked, unconsciously tightening her grip on his hand. This was what she had feared the most—that he would come in and take over everything.

"What if we turned the farm into a camp for underprivileged kids?"

She relaxed and sat back, smiling. "Jo said the same thing."

"Jo and I talked about it a lot our last few visits. I think it was what she wanted, but she didn't want to push her agenda on you."

"But I think it's a great idea," she said. "I've been giving it a lot of thought ever since she brought it up."

"What have you come up with?" he asked, smiling at the excitement in her tone.

She launched into a long explanation of what she wanted to do. He added his own thoughts, many of which overlapped or expanded on hers. They spent the entire three hours talking about the future of their charity, each one feeling a feverish excitement for what was to come. But when they pulled into town, Genevieve sobered.

"Darcy, I want you to take me home," she said.

"But I thought…" he trailed off, looking crestfallen.

She shook her head, refusing to look at him for fear she might give in and change her mind. "I'll work with you. We'll be partners, but only in business. I won't live at Jo's with you, and I won't marry you. We'll keep things strictly professional."

Silently, he drove to her rental house and parked, carrying her bags to her door and depositing them inside. She thought maybe he was angry, but when she turned to face him, he was smiling.

"You can live here and say you won't marry me, but good luck keeping things strictly professional. I love you, and sooner or later you're going to say yes when I ask you to marry me." He bent and kissed her before she could reply or protest. Like usual, she responded to him, totally forgetting the vow she had made a few minutes ago in the car. Instead she dropped her overnight bag and wrapped her arms around him, drawing him closer.

With a chuckle, Darcy broke the kiss and pulled away. "If that's your definition of keeping things professional, I like it mighty fine." He bestowed one more kiss on her forehead and let himself out, whistling as he walked away.

Frustrated, Genevieve closed the door harder than she intended, slamming it so it rattled its hinges. She leaned against the door and closed her eyes, fighting a wave of resignation. She might as well admit it: she was going to marry Darcy. Part of her felt relieved at finally letting go of her denial. She was tempted to open the door, call him back, and ask for her ring. But she didn't.

True, she loved him. Also true, she was eventually going to marry him. But along with that knowledge came the stinging reminder of his rejection. Maybe she was being petty or vindictive, but she didn't think the time had come to give in to his demands. If she gave in now so easily, she might spend the rest of her life bowing to his strong personality and indomitable spirit. Plus, saying yes right now didn't feel right.

In the end, she decided to wait and trust her instincts. Somehow she was sure she would know when the time was right.

For the next few weeks, Darcy and Genevieve worked seamlessly together. Since she was once again an employee of the Honeywell endowment, Darcy gave her the van. Though she would never admit it to him, she was ecstatic not to have to ride her bike to the farm anymore. The blind, hairpin turns had been terrifying and the hill so steep it had sapped what little energy she had. Now she could hop in the van and be there in less than ten minutes.

She arrived every morning at the same time. They mucked stalls together, fed and checked the horses, and she made breakfast. Genevieve was more relieved than she could say to have him there seeing to the horses' care. When he left the first time, he had hired a local to check on them, but the man had constantly plied Genevieve with questions she couldn't answer. While Jo had been alive, Genevieve could defer all questions to her, but she had been nervous about what would happen after Jo's death. Above everything, she wanted to keep the horses well and safe. Now she had Darcy to do that, and it was a huge weight off her shoulders.

She was also relieved not to have to handle the financial end of things. She was a mess with money, preferring to pay cash for everything rather than risk running into debt. Ever since her parents died, she'd had a vague sense of financial insecurity, as if her world might collapse around her and she would be tossed into debtor's prison if she was late paying a bill. For that reason she had kept her monthly bills as low as possible, forgoing cable, a car, phone, and many other luxuries. Not that she had been able to afford any of those things anyway. Her previous salary had been so far below the poverty level that she had qualified for food stamps and government healthcare. She hadn't taken advantage of the food stamps, but she had tapped into the healthcare when she discovered she had leukemia. Even so, it hadn't been enough to pay for all the treatments she required. Without Jo's assistance, Genevieve would literally be dead.

To Genevieve's surprise, Darcy seemed to be giving her space and honoring her request. Not that he didn't ask her to marry him every day, because he did, but he didn't kiss her goodnight or try to force his attentions on her. He hadn't even held her hand since he brought her back from his parents' house. And Genevieve missed him. Knowing Darcy, it was probably all part of some master plan, which made it all the more irksome that it was working. How was it that the man who proclaimed his undying love for her hadn't touched her in weeks, despite the fact that they spent all day every day together?

Finally, when she couldn't take it anymore, she sat on the couch after supper, moodily crossing and uncrossing her arms over her chest.

"Something wrong, Genevieve?" Darcy asked as he slowly scrolled through the channels.

"How come you don't kiss me anymore?" she blurted.

"Because you told me not to," he said, not removing his eyes from the television.

"Since when do you do what I tell you?" she asked. Trying to control Darcy was like trying to tame an electric current.

He tossed the remote onto the coffee table and looked at her. "Are you going to marry me?"

She shook her head.

"Then it seems we're at an impasse," he said, unconsciously mimicking her pose when he crossed his arms over his chest.

They stared at each other in a silent faceoff while the tension grew between them. At last she spoke. "You know what the best way to overcome an impasse is?"

He shook his head.

"Build a bridge," she said. She edged toward him, nudging aside his arms until she was in his embrace.

"What are you doing?" he asked.

"I'm kissing you. Who says I have to wait on you to make the first move? That's not a very feminist thing to do."

"Not with the feminist talk agai--," he said, but he couldn't finish his statement because she kissed him.

CHAPTER 22

*D*arcy was cooking his own supper and trying not to wallow in loneliness. Genevieve was only gone for the day, but he still missed her. He tried not to begrudge the part of her job that took her away from him, but it wasn't easy. She met weekly with the kids from the hospital to offer counseling sessions and talk about anything that was going on in their lives.

When the phone rang, he lunged for it, hoping it might be Genevieve calling to say she would be home soon. Then he spied her cell phone sitting on the table, the one he had bought for her in case of emergencies, the one she constantly forgot to take with her.

"Hello," he said probably sounding severe because he was irritated with Genevieve's forgetfulness. He didn't know where her mind was lately.

"I'm looking for Mr. Darcy Honeywell," a professional-sounding voice said.

"This is Darcy Honeywell," he replied, vaguely curious. Except for his family, no one knew where he was. Why would anyone be calling him?

"Mr. Honeywell, I work at the satellite extension of Children's Hospital here in Lawrence."

"Yes," Darcy said, gripping the phone tighter. "My fiancée is there today. Is she okay? Did something happen?"

"Well, yes, actually it did, though I wasn't aware Genevieve was engaged. She has you listed as her employer and emergency contact."

"I'm all of those things," Darcy said, fear making him impatient.

"Yes, of course, sorry, the reason I'm calling is because Genevieve lost consciousness after her treatment, and she's in no condition to drive herself home. If I had known she was driving herself, I never would have…"

"What?" Darcy roared, gripping the phone so that it actually made a creaking sound as if it were about to snap in half. "What treatment?"

There was a significant pause. "She didn't tell you?"

"Tell me what? She's there to meet with the kids for their counseling sessions."

"Oh, oh, bother. I'm treading on some thin ethical ice here," the woman said.

"Listen, lady, tell me what the problem is, or I swear you don't want to know what will happen if you don't."

"Genevieve has been taking her chemotherapy here the last couple of weeks. She arranged to have it at the same time as some of the kids she works with so she wouldn't have to drive to Lexington."

"Genevieve's leukemia is in remission," Darcy said.

"Not anymore," the woman said softly. "I'm sorry."

She might have said more, but Darcy didn't stay on the phone long enough to find out. Instead he grabbed his keys and sprinted out the door, taking the hairpin curves so fast that only years of driving experience kept his vehicle on the road. He was going to kill her, really and truly kill her. How could she not have told him something so monumental? And how could he have missed it? He, who spent every day with her, who had watched her working happily alongside him as if she hadn't a care in the world. How could he say he loved her if he didn't know her well enough to realize her cancer had returned? And how could she love him if she didn't bother to share such vital information?

He arrived at the satellite hospital much faster than he should have, pushing open the door so hard that he heard a cracking noise. Absently, he made a mental note to pay for it if it was broken. First things first, he was going to let Genevieve have it.

But when he arrived in the appropriate room, he realized she'd already had it. She was once again gray, tinged with shades of green, and looking more miserable than any human should. A woman was pressing a cloth to her forehead and taking her pulse.

"Is she conscious?" Darcy whispered.

The woman turned to look at him in alarm. "Yes."

He recognized her voice from the phone and went forward, holding out his hand. "Darcy Honeywell. I apologize if I was abrupt on the phone. As you can imagine, you took me by surprise and scared me."

"It's okay," she said. She rose and moved out of the way so Darcy could sit down. He did so, gathering Genevieve gently close so he could press his ear to her chest. The faint thrum of her heartbeat was less reassuring than he'd hoped for, and he felt panic clawing at the back of his throat.

Genevieve's eyes fluttered open. "Uh-oh," she whispered when she saw him.

"Uh-oh is right," he whispered. "The jig is up."

As Genevieve started to cry, the other woman slipped unobtrusively from the room. Darcy crawled into the uncomfortable little bed beside Genevieve, holding her as close and as tight as he dared, trying to fight back tears of his own. He tangled his hands in her hair and held her, rocking slightly back and forth.

"Genevieve, how could you not tell me?" he asked at last.

"Because I didn't want it to be true, Darcy. Everything has been so perfect. I thought if I didn't mention it, then it would go away."

He had the fear that she wasn't telling the exact truth, but he didn't know why he should suspect otherwise.

"You know what this means, don't you?" he asked.

She shook her head, still keeping her eyes closed.

"This means you're moving into Jo's house so I can take care of you."

"No," she wailed.

"Why not?"

"Because people will gossip," she said.

"I don't care," he said.

"I do. Plus, I don't want you to see what's about to happen."

"Genevieve, this isn't up for debate. And you could stop any gossip before it starts if you'll say yes and marry me."

She smiled slightly against his chest. "Low blow, Darcy, asking a girl when her defenses are down."

"Now is the best possible time to say yes," he said.

"Now is the worst possible time," she retorted.

"At least admit you love me," he pressed.

"I'm not saying I love you when I'm this close to throwing up," she told him.

"You're stubborn even when you're weak," he noted. "What's wrong with me that I find that attractive?"

Genevieve laughed and groaned. "Don't make me laugh, Darcy. I'm seriously about to lose it here."

"Sweetheart, I've had my hands inside a thousand horses. Believe me when I tell you that a little throw up isn't the worst thing that's ever been on my shirt."

"You are really, really bad at tending to sick people," Genevieve accused.

"I'll get better," Darcy said sincerely, smoothing his palm up and down her back. "I promise."

"You shouldn't have to," she said, so low he could barely hear her.

"I love you, Genevieve, and this is what love looks like. That's why they write it into the vows. You would know that if you would actually take them with me."

She laughed, but she was crying again.

"What's wrong?' he asked, knowing as he did so that it was a stupid question. "What hurts?" he amended.

"Everything. It's all awful."

"What can I do to make it better?" he asked, sounding as desperate as he felt.

"This. Hold me, Darcy," she said, gripping his shirt weakly in her hands.

"I can do this, Genevieve, as long as you want. Forever, if that's what it takes." Even as he said the words he realized forever might be a very short time.

$\mathcal{A}$ week later Darcy and Genevieve went to Thanksgiving at his parents' house. They had debated not going, but Genevieve didn't want to take him away from his family celebration, and Darcy thought the outing might do her some good. She had already lost five pounds she couldn't afford to lose, and her hair was beginning to thin. The grayness of her pallor wouldn't go away, and it was a constant reminder of her renewed illness.

The change of scene seemed to be working wonders for Genevieve because she was in high spirits. Then again, she was always in high spirits as far as Darcy could tell. Since the initial day he'd found out about her illness, she hadn't once complained about it, even though she had no appetite, was weak, and exhausted most of the time. She approached life with her usual pep and zest, even arguing with him when he had gone to her house to move her things.

"This isn't necessary, Darcy. I don't need to move into Jo's with you. I can take care of myself."

"Sure, you can," he said as she sat on her couch, too weak to do more than put up a futile protest. Since then he had taken over cooking duties because, even though she had tried to keep it up, she lacked the energy. And they were both suffering his failures. Unlike his brother Corliss, Darcy had no idea what to do in the kitchen. Thinking of Corliss gave him an idea and he vowed to speak to him, requesting that he come and fill the freezer with meals so they only had to pop something in the oven every night. Corliss loved to cook, and he didn't get much opportunity to do so because his parents' housekeeper did it on a daily basis.

Today, however, his mother had cooked. She was an excellent cook, but she was also very busy, working on the farm and overseeing a few charities in town. She didn't often cook for her large brood, so when she did it was a special treat. She always cooked Thanksgiving, and it was always delicious. Darcy smiled happily as he scanned the room. He loved Genevieve and the life he was building with her, but he also missed his family and was happy to be home. He wondered if he was destined to feel forever torn between the two.

His smile rested on Genevieve and slowly died. She looked frail and pale, as if a stiff wind could knock her over. And she was picking at her food, pushing it around on her plate without actually eating it. Every once in a while she would take a bite and grimace. As Darcy studied her, he was reminded of the horses after they got a mouthful of foxtail. It was almost like her mouth hurt, but she wouldn't keep that information from him, would she? He rolled his eyes. Of course she would—she was Genevieve, the woman who believed complaining was a cardinal sin.

"Genevieve, may I see you in the kitchen, please?" Darcy asked.

Genevieve slowly pushed out her chair while Darcy did the same. The family continued their various discussions, trying not to notice the two people leaving the room. They reached the deserted kitchen and Darcy whirled on Genevieve.

"Open your mouth," he commanded.

"Why?" she asked, backing away.

He captured her and set her on a high stool. "Because I said so. You know you're not leaving until you do it, so you might as well get it over with."

She did so, wincing and closing her eyes as the cool air hit her mouth.

Darcy had seen a lot of things during his medical training, but the sight of so many ulcerations on Genevieve's tongue, cheeks, and gums, still made him have to fight his gag reflex, probably because he knew how miserable she was.

"Genevieve, why didn't you tell me about this?" he yelled, so upset he was unable to keep his voice down.

She shrugged. "It's not that big of a deal, Darcy. It happened last time. I have to get used to it again."

"You don't have to get used to it; there are treatments for this. Why would you make yourself suffer this way? Stop being such a martyr." He opened the refrigerator and removed a can of meal replacement formula he had been force-feeding her for the last week. Fishing through drawers, he finally located a straw and shoved it in the opening.

"Tonight I'm going to treat you like I treat my horses when they have mouth sores," he said.

"You're going to curry my fur and feed me raisins?" she interrupted.

He ignored her. "We're going to do a saline rinse and then I'm going to apply a soothing paste I concocted, though I need to check a few things to make sure it's safe for humans. I'm pretty sure it is. First thing tomorrow, we're going to call your doctor and get a prescription to take care of this. In the mean time, you're going to drink at least three of those things a day." He pointed to the can in her hand.

Genevieve grimaced. She hated the meal replacement elixir. "You're bossy."

"You've made me this way," he thundered. Grasping her biceps, he tried to lower his voice. "You cannot hold out on me like this, Genevieve. We're partners. I'm trying to take care of you. Don't make my job harder. You have to keep me informed on every aspect of your care. Please."

She smoothed her hands over his cheeks. They were already stubbly, even though he had shaved two hours before. He was growing hair at an alarming rate while she was losing it at the same pace. "I want our last few months to be peaceful," she said gently.

"What?" he shouted so loudly that Grant poked his head around the corner of the kitchen before slowly backing away. "What are you talking about?"

"Darcy, you know the survival rate for this form of leukemia. It was amazing I made it through the first time. A recurrence doesn't usually end well."

"You're not dying, Genevieve," Darcy said. "You can't."

"I can, and I think I am," she said gently.

He backed away from her, shaking his head. "No. I won't allow it."

"I'm not sure there's anything you can do to change it," Genevieve said, hating to see him in so much pain. He looked wild, like a grizzly caught in a trap, not able to understand why his strength and determination was suddenly useless.

"Listen to me," he said urgently, stepping forward to lightly grip her biceps again. He had to force his grip to remain gentle when what he really wanted to do was shake her, but even the lightest touch left bruises that didn't fade. "You are not dying. I don't want to hear you say those words again. Ever. Do you understand? Don't say them to me ever, Genevieve. Ever."

She did understand because he looked ready to break. She couldn't say them to him again and watch him in this kind of pain, so she vowed to simply keep her thoughts to herself concerning her illness, which was ironic because previously he had told her to be open with him regarding her leukemia.

"Okay, Darcy, I won't tell you again," she said.

He shuddered at the cryptic note in her tone, moving forward to hold her close. His Adam's apple bobbed convulsively against her temple as he tried to get himself back under control.

"Darcy," she whispered.

"What?" he asked.

"I love you."

He laughed, easing away from her to cup her face. "You choose to tell me that for the first time now when I'm having the worst moment of my life?"

"You look like you need to hear it. Plus, I really do love you." She smiled and leaned up to press a soft kiss to his lips, wincing when the pressure was too much.

They rested their foreheads together. "Genevieve, sometimes I think you purposely look for ways to aggravate me, you know that? You finally tell me you love me when you know I can't kiss you senseless. Good thing I'm a man with such a patient and even temperament."

Genevieve laughed because the description didn't fit him at all. "Yes, Darcy, truly you have the patience of a saint. That's why you made that nurse cry last week."

"She wasn't being gentle with you," he said, still peeved at the way Nurse Ratchet had manhandled Genevieve when she'd been so ill.

"Lucky for me I'm able to see through all your bluster and realize that you truly are a good man," she said.

"Does that mean you're going to marry me now?" he asked.

She shook her head.

"C'mon, Genevieve. I'll give you good insurance coverage." He wagged his eyebrows at her.

"Charmer," Genevieve said.

The remainder of their Thanksgiving vacation was pleasant and fun. The medication for Genevieve's mouth didn't start working in time for her to be able to enjoy any delicious Thanksgiving food, but it did begin to ease a little of her misery, making her feel stupid that she hadn't mentioned the problem beforehand. She had no idea why she sometimes felt it was her duty to suffer in silence; she just did.

The Honeywells were always fun, but they seemed even more so now, and Genevieve wondered if it was for her benefit or maybe Darcy's. Darcy seemed to be struggling with his own dark mood. He would begin to sink, and one of his brothers would know what to say to pull him back out again. They were even getting along with Coy, playing football together without ganging up on him and trying to kill him. Genevieve wasn't sure, but she thought that might be a first.

Ivy's pregnant belly was beginning to burgeon over her pants, and this was her last visit to Kentucky before her baby was born. Haley was also making a lot of trips to the bathroom. Everyone waited with baited breath for her to announce her pregnancy, but either she wasn't or she and Brent had deemed it too early to tell people. Or, more likely, Haley hadn't told Brent yet. He still seemed as clueless as ever, though he clearly adored his young wife.

Baby Keeley was beginning to roll over, and Allie was beginning to get her energy back. She and Genevieve spent a long time talking about the charity foundation. Allie was a lawyer who did some pro bono work at a firm in Lexington, but she was interested in helping people before they ran into trouble with the law. The two women talked a lot about society's ills and what needed to be done. For Genevieve, it was a refreshing change from the constancy of thinking about her illness.

All in all it was a perfect weekend. Genevieve began to feel optimistic about her illness. Maybe she would make it through this time again. After all, it would be cruel to have found so much happiness only to lose it again so quickly. She simply had to buckle down, get through her treatments, and try to eat enough to keep herself alive. How difficult could any of that be? She would soon learn that the answer was "very."

CHAPTER 24

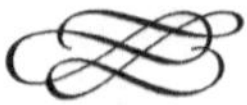

*D*arcy and Genevieve stayed home for Christmas. Not only because Genevieve was too sick and weak for a big celebration, but also because the remainder of the Honeywell clan went to Montana to celebrate with Ivy and Coy.

"I would like to see Montana," Genevieve said wistfully.

"I'll take you when you're better," Darcy promised. "Don't tell the Yankee I said so, but it really is beautiful country. Not as pretty as Kentucky, but still," he added loyally. "We could honeymoon there, but you'd have to marry me first." He gave her a squeeze.

She smiled, surveying the opened presents scattered around the room. They were more fit for someone three times her age. Everything spoke of comfort, from the heated mattress pad to the slippers and wool socks to the cozy sweaters and flannel pajamas. Genevieve dared not laugh at them, though, for fear of hurting Darcy's feelings. The gifts weren't romantic, but she knew Darcy was concerned about her inability to get warm and stay that way. Even now bundled in an afghan and wrapped in his arms, she was shivering, and the shivers were exhausting. She felt worse than usual today, and she wondered why. Hopefully it didn't mean anything at all.

Darcy's mother called a few minutes later, and by the time they finished their greeting, Genevieve was asleep. Darcy stared at her with a worried frown as his mother filled him in on all the news from Montana. Genevieve was acting odd, subdued and lifeless, with chills that wracked her body. Her treatments were progressing well, her blood work was looking better, but the danger was always that she would catch something that could ravage her already weakened immune system. Darcy was meticulous about washing his hands and keeping her out of public places but Genevieve, being Genevieve, wasn't one for being kept inside. He was thankful she had scheduled her chemo treatments with the kids she counseled. She provided therapy for them, listening to what was happening in their lives, but he thought it was good therapy for her, too. Being helpful was what made Genevieve feel good, and she was definitely helping the kids with whom she took chemo. Darcy went with her and watched as she eased their anxiety and made them laugh, diverting them from what was happening to their bodies.

As he hung up with his mother, his thoughts returned to Genevieve and the possibility of an illness. Now was the worst possible time for her to get sick because a blizzard was on its way. As remote as they were, getting proper medical treatment might prove impossible. They could be snowed in for days. Darcy chastised himself for not taking her to his parents' empty house for the holiday, but he hadn't wanted the long car ride to tax her.

Sometimes he felt like he was striking blind, trying desperately to do what was best for her with no idea what he was doing. And Genevieve wasn't much help. She refused to complain about anything, which made her a pleasant patient, but left him with no idea how she was feeling. If not for her lethargy and physical appearance, one might never know she was ill.

He woke her and helped her to bed, tucking the covers up tight and kissing her forehead when he realized she was already asleep again. He backed out of the room, once again thinking he needed a baby monitor. Genevieve would balk, but it would be worth it for Darcy to have peace of mind while she slept. As it was, he slept fitfully, imagining every little sound was her. Twice he bolted out of bed thinking he heard her, but when he checked she was safely asleep in her bed.

The third time, he was sure it was her, and he was correct. She stood in the living room, frantically tossing pillows from the couch.

"Genevieve," he exclaimed. She looked up at him with fever-bright eyes that didn't really see him. "What are you doing, sweetheart?"

"I can't find it," she said.

"Find what?" he asked.

"The box," she replied, beginning her frantic search again. Realizing she had no idea what she was doing, Darcy went forward and gripped her wrists. His touch was gentle, but it set Genevieve off so that she began screaming and flailing like a wild thing. Shocked, Darcy wrapped his arms protectively around her to keep her from hurting herself, and that's when he realized she was burning up. If he had to guess, he would say her fever was at least a hundred four degrees or higher. The icy edge of panic that was his constant companion lately gripped his heart, rendering him incapable of thought for a few minutes.

She hadn't stopped fighting him, despite the fact that her arms were pinned. She was exhausting herself, using up energy she didn't have to spare in the first place. He grabbed the cordless phone and planted Genevieve on the couch, pressing his body over hers to stop her from flailing. For whatever reason, it worked and she began to relax. Her breathing sounded labored, though he didn't know if it was because she was ill or because he was crushing her. He adjusted his position, giving her more room to breath, but she still sounded as if she was wheezing through liquid.

Trying to force himself to remain calm, he squinted at the phone and dialed 9-1-1. The operator came on the line and he told her the address. With a sinking heart, he listened as her tone changed from helpful to regretful.

"I'm sorry to say, sir, that our ambulances can't make it up your road or any of the other mountain roads right now."

"Do you think an SUV can make it down?" he asked, thankful for his four-wheel drive.

"At this point we're not recommending it. The county is under a level three snow emergency; that means only emergency vehicles are allowed on the road, but even our emergency vehicles can't make it up the hill. I apologize sir. I'm authorized to give you emergency medical instructions over the phone if that helps."

"It doesn't," Darcy said, trying not to take out his frustration on her.

"Road crews are working as hard as possible. We're hoping all roads will be passable by tomorrow if you can hang on that long."

"I'm not the one who needs to hang on that long," he said, disconnecting the call. *Think, Darcy, think,* he commanded himself. What he needed to do was think like a doctor and stop thinking like Genevieve's boyfriend. What would he do if one of the horses was this sick? What would be his priority? Bringing down her fever seemed to be the immediate concern. Genevieve was out of her head hallucinating, and she was beginning to thrash beneath him again.

He closed his eyes, resting his forehead against the couch for a moment. "Okay," he said out loud. "This is going to be fine. We can do this. Genevieve is going to be fine." Saying the words out loud gave him the reassurance he needed to believe them. He left her on the couch, still thrashing and moaning as he went to search the cupboards for medication. Finding none, he slammed the cupboards shut in frustration. How could he not have thought to have medication on hand for such an emergency?

He thought of his medical bag in the bedroom, the one he carried for horse emergencies, and went to his room to search it. As he hurried down the hall, he tried to make a mental list of what was inside and what could be used on humans, but he couldn't think clearly. Grabbing the bag, he sprinted back to the family room and dropped it onto the coffee table, peering inside. Like a beacon of hope, he finally located a glass bottle of oxytetracycline, an antibiotic used to treat fever in horses. It was a human drug, but he would have to administer the right dosage and inject Genevieve, two things that made him nervous. He tried to weigh the pros and cons of treating her versus not treating her, but his brain was too muddled by panic to think clearly. He decided to go with his first instinct, and his gut was telling him to dose her. The drug was safe unless she had an allergy. At the most it would cause her mild intestinal discomfort, but that had to be better than being out of her head with fever and thrashing so wildly on the couch Darcy thought maybe she was having a febrile seizure.

The thought that she might be seizing renewed his panic and also his determination. Guessing her weight to be somewhere around eighty pounds now, he loaded up enough antibiotic for a foal and injected it into her thigh, then he carried her to her bed and retrieved a cool washcloth, removing her clothes so he could reach as much of her as possible. After about a half hour, the fever broke. Darcy redressed her in a fresh gown and tucked the covers around her. In the morning, he would change her sheets. For now, he was too tired. He lay beside her, on top of the covers so he wouldn't get so warm he was tempted to sleep, and then he began his vigil, watching her for any further signs of distress. Someday he hoped this would be an interesting anecdote in their lives. He comforted himself by pretending to tell the story to their future children. Kids would probably find it funny that he had given her a shot of horse drugs, and he would let them laugh, never revealing how frightened he had been that she was going to die.

Thinking the word caused him to wince and squeeze his eyes tightly closed. "Genevieve is going to be fine," he said out loud. "She's going to get through this and live a long, healthy life."

He left her to retrieve his medical bag and used his stethoscope to listen to her heart and lungs, pinching his eyes closed again when he heard how weak her heartbeat was and how much fluid was in her lungs. If she had pneumonia, oxytetracycline would help. He would keep dosing her until he could get her to a hospital.

Opening his eyes, he took a deep breath, then another, and another, knowing the only way either of them was going to survive this horrible and scary night was one breath at a time.

CHAPTER 25

Genevieve opened her eyes and blinked in surprise at Darcy's sleeping form. As if he sensed she was awake, his eyes flew open and quickly scanned her up and down. Assuring himself she was okay, he settled back against his pillow and smiled.

"Good morning."

"Good morning," she replied. "Why are you in my bed, and why are my clothes different?"

Darcy laughed, relief mixing with amusement so that his chuckle felt bone deep. "Eight of the worst hours of my life just passed, and you're worried about your modesty. Prude. To answer your question, you've been sick. Last night wasn't so great. I had to wash you a few times and change your nightgown."

"You washed me? You changed me?" she asked, flushing.

"Yes, but if it makes you feel better, I was too panicked to have any recollection of what I was looking at. Of course, if you want to give me a refresher…" He reached for her and she wriggled away, laughing.

"Let's not do what people already think we're doing up here. I still have to face your mother, you know. I'd like to be able to look her in the eye when I do."

Darcy rolled his eyes, but he was smiling. His relief was palpable. "How do you feel?"

Genevieve's weak smile faded. "Not great, actually. What do you suppose is wrong with me?"

"If you were my horse, I would say pneumonia, but you should probably get a second opinion from a people doctor. As soon as the roads clear, I'm taking you to the hospital."

She nodded, feeling worse by the second. "Darcy, I think I'm going to…" Clapping her hand over her mouth, she threw off the covers and sprinted for the bathroom, barely making it in time to retch into the toilet. To her chagrin, Darcy came before she was finished, pressing a cool cloth to the back of her neck.

"I need to lie down," she said weakly.

"Here or in your room?" he asked.

"Here," she said. She was pretty certain that wasn't the last time she was going to be sick.

Darcy lay beside her, pressing the cloth to her forehead. Genevieve laid her hand over his and closed her eyes. "I promised myself I would never let you see me like this," she said, sounding on the verge of tears. "This is horrible."

"This is nothing," he said. "Last night was horrible." At least now she was speaking to him. She might feel awful, but she was in her right mind. Nothing would ever rid him of the vision of her pitiful fever-induced thrashing. He had truly thought he might be watching her final death throes.

She turned to him with a smile. "I'm sorry you had to see that," she said, tracing the shadows under his eyes.

Darcy laughed and caught her hand. "Genevieve, only you would apologize for being sick. I wish you wouldn't. Can't you please be a little bit normal and think of yourself for once?"

"I'll try," she promised. "Someday soon I'll surprise you and be the most selfish girl on the planet, demanding diamond tiaras and mink furs."

"I can't buy you mink," he said. "Think how it would look for a vet to buy pelts."

"I'll think of something else then," she said.

"See that you do," he said, enjoying talking about nothing.

"So the roads are pretty bad, huh?" she asked.

"Horrible. But at least we haven't lost power."

Almost as soon as he finished speaking, the lights blinked and went off. After a few seconds of stunned surprise, Genevieve started to laugh. "Do you think it's possible that we're cursed?" she asked.

Darcy smiled, putting his arms around her and scooting her close. "At least we…" he began, but she covered his mouth with her fingers.

"Better not say it; lightning may come down from the sky and strike us. Let's appreciate the darkness and silence for a while. I bet it's beautiful outside."

They lay quietly for a few minutes. Genevieve's stomach was still rioting, and she lacked the energy to move, but she wasn't worried. She felt certain that she had passed through the worst of whatever was wrong with her while she was out of her head and Darcy was standing watch. The lights flicked back on.

"That's odd," Genevieve said. "I've never known the power company to work that quickly before. Maybe they were already in the area."

Darcy shook his head. "It's the generator," he replied, sounding as sleepy as he looked.

"Jo had a generator?"

"No, I had it installed when I moved in here. I also bought a whole bunch of emergency supplies. We have enough food, water, and heat for a couple of weeks."

She blinked at him in surprise. "You did all that?"

"I'm a man, Genevieve. It's what we do; we take care of the ones we love."

And with that statement, Genevieve knew it was the right time to say yes. "Darcy," she whispered.

"Hmm," he answered, already half asleep.

"Ask me to marry you again."

His eyes flapped open like roller shades. "Now?"

"Now."

"Hold on," he said. He stood, dashed to his bedroom, and returned with the ring. Lying down beside her again, he opened the box to reveal a stunningly beautiful diamond and sapphire arrangement. "Dr. Porter, will you marry me?"

"Why yes, Dr. Honeywell, I believe I will." She held out her left hand, so weak that it shook while he slipped the ring on. He bent to kiss her, but she held up a hand. "Could you maybe help me brush my teeth first?"

"Okay." He helped her stand and held her over the sink while she brushed her teeth. Then he laid her back down, brushed his teeth, and lay down beside her again. And then he kissed her, more gently than he wanted because she was still so weak.

"After all these months I've been proposing to you, please don't tell me it was a generator that finally tipped the scales in my direction," he said when the kiss was finished.

"I'm afraid so."

"Why?"

"Because when we first met, I thought I was at my worst. And you didn't want me. But this," she paused and looked around the bathroom, "this is definitely me at my worst. And not only are you still here, but you're taking care of me. And not just the day to day taking care of me, but providing for the big things, too, like generators and food for when the weather gets bad. I haven't had that kind of provision since I was eighteen, and to have found it in you, Darcy, whom I love so much, is too good to be true. Thanks for being patient with me while I came around."

"Some things are worth waiting for, Genevieve," Darcy replied. "Before we go to the hospital, there's one thing you need to know about becoming a Honeywell."

"What's that?" she asked.

"If you want something, then you go out and get it, and don't let anything stop you until you do. That's the Honeywell way, and that's what you're going to have to become if I marry you. No more thinking this is the end of you. You're going to make it through this illness, and you're not going to die until I say you can. Is that clear?"

"I think you might be right. I think I'm going to beat this and have those twelve babies you promised."

"I dunno about that. If we have to wait five years, we might need to knock that number down to six."

"I was promised twelve, and I'm invoking the Honeywell way of thinking starting now. We're having twelve."

"We're going to have to double up and have some twins if we're going to make it," Darcy said.

"If you say so," she agreed.

Darcy smiled. "I do like a submissive woman."

"Then you've definitely come to the right place. I'm as submissive as they get."

"Sure you are," Darcy lied. "Now let's go celebrate our engagement with hospital food."

"Charmer," Genevieve said as Darcy scooped her from the floor. Easily hefting her into his arms, he bundled her up and stuck her in his car for the long drive to the hospital.

EPILOGUE

Seven months later, Darcy and Genevieve attended the Kentucky Derby. After Genevieve agreed to marry him, Darcy backed off his strict policy of only taking his wife to the event, saying that they could wait until she was fully recovered in order to be married. But once Genevieve made up her mind, she didn't want to wait. They were married the first week in April, a few days after Genevieve's final treatment. She hadn't lost all of her hair this time, though it had thinned considerably. A talented stylist was able to weave in some hairpieces, adding volume and luster to her thin, brittle hair. The same person also did her makeup, covering up her still sallow complexion and sunken cheeks. She was thinner than she wanted to be, but another talented person—the seamstress this time— filled in her dress with some cleverly hidden padding in all the right places.

Now, a little over a month past her wedding and final treatment, Genevieve looked like a new person. Her hair had filled in, and so had her body. Her complexion was a rosy picture of perfect health, and her smile was no longer forced. She wanted to say she felt good, but she couldn't. For some reason, she didn't think she was bouncing back as quickly as she should.

Though she hadn't said anything to Darcy, he still insisted she go to the doctor as soon as they left the derby.

"How did you know I wasn't feeling well?" she asked.

"Because last week when we were building the cabin, you didn't insist on climbing up to the top and hammering anything," Darcy replied. He and his brothers had been working on building not only two cabins, but also a mess tent for their new camp. The work was finished, and the grand opening of the Josephine Honeywell Horse Camp was set for the following week, which was good because the entire summer was already booked with campers. A handful of people from the community had been hired to help with the food and animals, and kids in youth groups from all over the country were coming in to work as volunteer counselors, though Genevieve would be overseeing any actual counseling.

Now they waited nervously in the doctor's office, and when he returned grim-faced and holding a sheet of paper, their stomachs sank, fearing the worst.

"Genevieve, I thought I impressed on you the importance of using birth control for a while," were the doctor's first words.

"You did," Genevieve said. "We've been extremely careful."

"Not careful enough," the doctor said, exasperated. "I know how you feel about children, but my recommendation is an immediate termination. Your body isn't recovered enough to handle a pregnancy. This is going to compromise your already compromised systems. If you choose to go through with this pregnancy, you could die, and so could your baby."

Genevieve tried not to get upset with her doctor by reminding herself he was trying to do what he thought was in her best interest. Of course he wouldn't understand that it could never be in her best interest to do away with her child, but thankfully Darcy did.

"I'm keeping the baby," Genevieve said. "And she's going to be fine. She's a Honeywell, and if she can somehow be conceived despite all our precautions, she must really want to be born. Who am I to take that away from her?"

The doctor again gave all his reasons for terminating the pregnancy, and while many of them were probably valid, Genevieve didn't listen.

"I appreciate your concern, but this is not up for discussion. I want this baby, and she wants to be born. There's no stopping it," Genevieve said. The doctor was looking at her like she was crazy, and maybe she was, but she had come to believe Darcy's philosophy that if she wanted something badly enough all she had to do to get it was to not take no for an answer. She hadn't planned to be pregnant, but now that she was, nothing was going to stop her from carrying it to completion.

She and Darcy left the doctor's office, feeling shell-shocked despite their joy. "I guess we should start looking at N names," Darcy said. Since Ivy had a Lucy, and Haley was having a Macy, "N" would be their designated letter.

"I already have a name picked out," Genevieve said. "Nasya. It's Hebrew, and it means miracle of God."

"Nasya," Darcy repeated. "I like that."

They rode in silence for a little while, trying to process how drastically their lives were about to change. "What happens when someone reaches the end of the alphabet?" Genevieve asked at last. "Do you have to start doubling letters? Are we someday going to have a little niece or nephew 'Aardvark'?"

"I don't know," Darcy said, sounding worried. "My brothers, Ivy, and I have never talked about what happens then."

"Maybe if we hurry, we can use all twelve remaining letters before Grant and Everett get married," Genevieve said. "Then it will be their problem."

Darcy laughed. "I think we can take our time. According to Everett, he's never getting married, and Grant is, well, Grant. You know."

She did. Grant was loveable, but maturity wasn't exactly a shining character trait. "Stranger things have happened. For instance, I married you. Did you know before I met you I had a height limit? There was a time when I wouldn't date anyone over 5'10". Now I sort of wish I'd stuck with that. This baby is going to be folded into quarters by the time she comes out."

"You're sure it's going to be a girl?" Darcy asked. "All the grandchildren so far have been girls. We're about due for a boy."

"No, it's going to be a girl."

"Maybe she'll be tiny like you," Darcy suggested.

"Maybe," Genevieve said hopefully. "But she's performed a miracle by being alive; I'm not going to expect anything else of her."

Eight months later, Nasya Honeywell was perfectly healthy. And, at five pounds and five ounces, she was the smallest Honeywell baby on record for as long as the family had been keeping track.

T hank you for reading *Wild Pride,* book three in the Honeywells of Kentucky series. For more books, please check out my website at www.vanessagraybartal.com